WI

"Love is always a weapon, Bennet."

"It doesn't have to be," he replied steadfastly, his blue eyes an odd shade in the light of the laptop screen.

Alyssa's chest felt tight, and her heart felt too much like it was being squeezed. She'd wanted to feel something, but not this. Not anything to do with love.

Before Alyssa realized what he was doing, Bennet had his hand fisted in her shirt and tugged her down. Then his mouth was on hers. Gentle, and something that kind of made her want to cry because there'd been so little of it in her life. His lips caressed hers, his tongue slowly tracing the outline of her bottom lip, and all she could do was soak it up...

STONE COLD CHRISTMAS RANGER

Nicole Helm

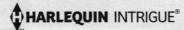

To late-night train whistles when everyone else is asleep and the Janette Oke books that introduced me to romance.

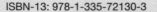

Recycling programs
for this product may
not exist in your area.

ISBN-13: 978-1-335-72130-3

Stone Cold Christmas Ranger

Copyright © 2017 by Nicole Helm

All rights reserved. Except for use in any review, the reproduction or utilization of this work in whole or in part in any form by any electronic, mechanical or other means, now known or hereinafter invented, including xerography, photocopying and recording, or in any information storage or retrieval system, is forbidden without the written permission of the publisher, Harlequin Enterprises Limited, 225 Duncan Mill Road, Don Mills, Ontario M3B 3K9, Canada.

This is a work of fiction. Names, characters, places and incidents are either the product of the author's imagination or are used fictitiously, and any resemblance to actual persons, living or dead, business establishments, events or locales is entirely coincidental.

This edition published by arrangement with Harlequin Books S.A.

For questions and comments about the quality of this book, please contact us at CustomerService@Harlequin.com.

® and TM are trademarks of Harlequin Enterprises Limited or its corporate affiliates. Trademarks indicated with ® are registered in the United States Patent and Trademark Office, the Canadian Intellectual Property Office and in other countries.

Printed in U.S.A.

HARLEQUIN®

equin.com

Nicole Helm grew up with her nose in a book and the dream of one day becoming a writer. Luckily, after a few failed career choices, she gets to follow that dream—writing down-to-earth contemporary romance and romantic suspense. From farmers to cowboys, Midwest to *the* West, Nicole writes stories about people finding themselves and finding love in the process. She lives in Missouri with her husband and two sons and dreams of someday owning a barn.

Books by Nicole Helm

Harlequin Intrigue

Stone Cold Texas Ranger
Stone Cold Undercover Agent
Stone Cold Christmas Ranger

Harlequin Superromance

A Farmers' Market Story

All I Have
All I Am

Falling for the New Guy
Too Friendly to Date
Too Close to Resist

Visit the Author Profile page at Harlequin.com.

CAST OF CHARACTERS

Bennet Stevens—Texas Ranger with the Unsolved Crimes Unit. From an influential, wealthy political family. Partners with Vaughn Cooper. Wants to solve the longest-running cold case his unit has.

Alyssa Jimenez—Grew up in a powerful drug-cartel family, but was kidnapped by The Stallion in her early twenties. Since her rescue, she's built a not-quite-legal bounty hunter business and lives in a garage apartment at her friend Gabby's house.

Gabby Torres—Alyssa's friend who's taken her in. They met when they were both separately kidnapped by The Stallion but held at the same place.

CJ Jimenez—Alyssa's oldest brother and current leader of the Jimenez drug cartel.

Oscar Jimenez—Alyssa's youngest brother, also part of the Jimenez drug cartel.

Lynette Stevens—Bennet's mother, a Texas state representative.

Gary L. Stevens—Bennet's father, a US senator.

Salvador Dominguez—Leader of the Dominguez drug cartel, which is encroaching on the Jimenezes' territory.

Vaughn Cooper—Bennet's Texas Ranger partner, getting ready to take a leave of absence.

Jaime Alessandro—Gabby's fiancé. FBI agent.

Chapter One

Bennet Stevens had learned how to smile politely and charmingly at people he couldn't stand before he'd learned to walk. Growing up in a family chock-full of lawyers and politicians, and many of the Texas rich and powerful, he'd been bred to be a charming, cunning tool.

His decision to go into police work had surprised, and perhaps not excited, his parents, but they weren't the type of people to stand in someone's way.

Everything was far more circumspect than that, and after five years as a Texas Ranger, easily moving up the ranks beyond his counterparts, Bennet was starting to wonder if *that's* how his parents were attempting to smoke him out.

Make everything too damn easy.

He was as tired of easy here at the Texas Rangers headquarters in Austin as he was of political parties at his parents' home where he was supposed to flirt with debutantes and impress stuffed suits with tales of his bravery and valor.

Which was why he was beyond determined to break one of the coldest cases his Texas Ranger unit had. The timing couldn't be more perfect, with his partner in the Unsolved Crimes Investigation Unit taking some extended time off giving Bennet the opportunity to solve a case on his own.

He glanced over at said partner, Ranger Vaughn Cooper, who was leaning against the corner of their shared office, talking on his cell in low tones.

No amount of low tones could hide the fact taciturn Ranger Cooper was talking to his very pregnant wife. Bennet could only shake his head at how the mighty had fallen, and hard.

Vaughn said his goodbyes and shoved his phone into his pocket before he turned his attention to Bennet, assessing gaze and hard expression back in place. "Captain won't go for it," Vaughn said, nodding at the file on Bennet's desk.

"He might if you back me up."

Vaughn crossed his arms over his chest, and if Bennet hadn't worked with Vaughn for almost four years, he might have been intimidated or worried. But that steely-eyed glare meant Vaughn was considering it.

"I know you want more…"

"But?" Bennet supplied, forcing himself to grin as if this didn't mean everything. When people knew what it meant, they crushed it if they could. Another Stevens lesson imparted early and often.

"I'm not sure this case is the way to go. It's been sitting here for years."

"I believe that's the point of our department. Besides that, I've already found a new lead," Bennet said, never letting the easy smile leave his face.

Vaughn's eyebrows rose in surprise. "You have?"

"There was a murder around the same time as this case that the FBI linked to the Jimenez drug cartel. That victim's wounds were the same as the victim's wounds in our Jane Doe case. If Captain lets me take on this case, I want to find a connection."

Vaughn blew out a breath and nodded. "You have the FBI file?"

Bennet turned his laptop screen so Vaughn could read. Vaughn's expression changed, just a fraction, and for only a second, but Bennet caught it. And jumped. "What? What did you see?"

Vaughn sighed heavily. "I didn't *see* anything. It's just…Jimenez."

"What about it?"

"Alyssa Jimenez."

"I know that name." Bennet racked his brain for how, because it hadn't been in any of the files he'd been poring over lately. "The Stallion. Oh, she was with Gabby." Vaughn's sister-in-law had been the kidnapping victim of a madman who called himself The Stallion. Vaughn had worked the case to free Gabby and the handful of other girls she'd been in captivity with.

Including Alyssa Jimenez. "Wait. Are you telling me *she* has something to do with the Jimenez drug family?"

"I don't know that she does. But based on what I do know, I wouldn't be surprised."

"But you haven't followed up?" Bennet asked incredulously.

"Natalie and Gabby took her in after Gabby's release. They've adopted her like a sister, and I have yet to see anything that points to her being involved with any of the many members of the Jimenez drug cartel family."

"But you think she is," Bennet pressed, because Vaughn wouldn't have brought it up if he didn't.

"Alyssa is…different. It wouldn't surprise me if she had connections to this family. She's built something of an underground bounty hunter business, and the contacts she has?" Vaughn shook his head. "I promised Gabby and Nat I wouldn't interfere unless it was directly part of my job."

"You? You, Mr. By-the-Book, promised not to investigate something?"

"She hasn't done anything wrong, and believe me, I've watched. *If* she's connected to that family, it's only biological. Not criminal. She's been through a lot."

"Wait. Wait. Isn't she the one who fought the FBI when they raided The Stallion's compound to release the women?"

Vaughn stood to his full height, disapproval written all over his face, but Bennet wouldn't let it stop him. Vaughn's family leave started tomorrow, and he couldn't stand in Bennet's way for weeks.

"She didn't fight them off. She just didn't exactly drop her weapon when they demanded her to do so. There is a difference. Now, Bennet, I need you to understand something."

Bennet held himself very still, especially since Vaughn rarely called him by his first name. They were partners, but Vaughn was older, more experienced, and Bennet had always looked up to him like something of a mentor.

"Do not let your need to do something big compromise your job, which is to do something *right*."

The lecture grated even though Bennet knew it was a good one, a fair one. But he didn't particularly want to be good or fair right now. He wanted to *do* something. He wanted a challenge. He wanted to feel less like this fake facade.

He would do all that by doing that something right, damn it. "I want her contact information."

"I didn't say I'd back you up. I didn't say—"

"I want her contact information," Bennet repeated, and this time he didn't smile or hide the edge in his voice. "I have found a lead that no one else has found, and I will rightfully and lawfully follow up on it once Captain Dean gives me the go-ahead. Now, you can either give it to me and smooth the way and let this be easy—for me *and* for her—or you can stand in my way and force me to drag her in here."

Vaughn's expression was icy, but Bennet couldn't worry about that. Not for this. So, he continued.

"You're out for a month to spend with your wife and your upcoming new addition. Take it. Enjoy it. And while you're gone, let me do my job the way I see fit."

Bennet couldn't read Vaughn's silence, but he supposed it didn't matter. Bennet had said his piece, and he'd made it very clear. He would not be dissuaded.

"If you get Captain Dean's go-ahead, I'll give you Gabby's contact information. It'll be the best way to get ahold of Alyssa."

When Bennet frowned, Vaughn's mouth curved into the closest it ever got to a smile on duty.

"Best of luck getting anything out of Gabby Torres."

Bennet forced himself to smile. "I can handle your sister-in-law." And he could handle this case, and the potential to crack it wide open. Starting with Alyssa Jimenez.

ALYSSA NEVER KNEW what to do when Gabby went into full protective mode. While Alyssa had grown up with five intimidating older brothers, they had protected her by throwing her in a room and locking the door, by teaching her to use any weapon she could get her hands on. They had protected her by hiding her.

Not ranting and raving about some half-cocked Texas Ranger wanting to talk to her.

Not that Alyssa needed Gabby's protection, but it was still interesting to watch.

"The *nerve* of that guy, thinking he can question you about something that doesn't even have anything to do with you!"

Alyssa sat with her elbows resting on her knees in a folding chair in the corner of her very odd little office. It was a foreclosed gas station in a crappy part of Austin, and Alyssa hadn't made any bones about making it look different from what it was. Shelves still stood in aisles, coolers stood empty and not running along the back wall. The only thing she'd done was add some seating—mostly stuff she'd found in the alley—and a desk that had a crack down the middle.

Her clientele didn't mind, and they knew where to find her without her having to advertise and attract potential…legal issues.

The only time the office space bothered Alyssa was when Gabby insisted on showing up. Even though Alyssa knew Gabby could take care of herself—she'd recently graduated from the police academy, and she'd survived eight years as a prisoner of The Stallion to Alyssa's two—Alyssa hated bringing people she cared about into this underworld.

"Alyssa. Are you listening?"

Alyssa shrugged. "Not really. You seem to be doing an excellent job of yelling all by yourself."

Gabby scowled at her, and it was moments like these Alyssa didn't know what to do with. Where it felt like she had a sister, a family. People who cared about her. It made her want to cry, and it made her want to…

She didn't know. So, she ignored it. "I can talk to some Texas Ranger. I talk to all sorts of people all the time." Criminals. Law enforcement. Men who worked for her brothers, men who worked for the FBI, including Gabby's fiancé. Alyssa knew how to talk to anyone.

Maybe, just maybe, it made her a little nervous someone so close to Natalie and Gabby had possibly discovered her connection to one of the biggest cartels operating in the state of Texas, but she could handle it.

"Crap," Gabby muttered, looking at her phone. "Nat went into labor."

"Well, hurry up and get to the hospital."

"Come with me."

"No."

"Alyssa, you're ours now. Really."

"I know," Alyssa replied, even though it had been almost two years since escaping The Stallion and she still wasn't used to being considered part of the family. "But all that pushing and yelling and weird baby crap? I'm going to have to pass. I'll come visit when it's all over, so keep me posted. Besides, I have some work to catch up on. My trip to Amarillo took longer than I expected."

She'd brought a rapist to justice. Though she'd brought him in for a far more minor charge, the woman who'd come to her for help could rest assured her attacker was in jail.

It wasn't legal to act as bounty hunter without a license, but growing up in the shadow of a drug cartel family, Alyssa didn't exactly care about legal. She cared about righting some wrongs.

Some of that pride and certainty must have showed in her expression because Gabby sighed. "All right, I won't fight you on it. Get your work done and then, regardless of baby appearance, at least stop by the hospital tonight?"

"Fine."

Gabby pulled her into a quick hug, another gesture Alyssa had spent two years not knowing what to do with. But the Torres sisters had pulled her in and insisted she was part of their family.

It mattered, and Alyssa would do whatever she could to make sure she made them proud. She couldn't be a police officer like Gabby, or a trained hypnotist assisting the Texas Rangers like Natalie, but she could do this.

"See you tonight," Gabby said, heading for the door.

"Yes, ma'am."

Gabby left, and Alyssa sighed. Maybe she should have gone. Natalie had had a difficult pregnancy, enough so that her husband was taking almost an entire month off work to be home with her and the baby the first few weeks. And, no matter how uncomfortable Alyssa still was with the whole child-birth thing, they were her family.

Her good, upstanding chosen family. *Who don't know who you really are.*

Alyssa turned to her work. There was some paper-work to forge to collect her fee for the last guy she'd brought in, and then she had to check her makeshift mailbox to see if any more tips had been left for her. She worked by word of mouth, mostly for people who couldn't pay, hence the forging paperwork so she could pretend to be a licensed bounty hunter and collect enough of a fee to live off of.

Her front door screeched open, as the hinges weren't aligned or well oiled. She glanced over ex-pecting to find a woman from the neighborhood, as those were usually her only word-of-mouth visitors.

Instead, a man stepped through the door, and for a few seconds Alyssa couldn't act, she could only stare. He was tall and broad, dressed in pressed khakis and a perfectly tailored button-down shirt, a Texas Ranger badge hooked to his belt. He wore a cowboy hat and a gun like he'd been born with them.

Alyssa's heart beat twice its normal rhythm, something unrecognizable fluttering in her chest. His dark hair was thick and wavy, and not buzzed short like most Texas Rangers she'd come into con-tact with. His eyes were a startling blue, and his mouth—

Wait. Why was she staring at his mouth?

The man's brows drew together as he looked

around the room. He cleared his throat. "I'm sorry, are you... You are Alyssa Jimenez, aren't you?"

"And you must be the Texas Ranger Gabby's trying to hide me from," Alyssa offered drily. "How *did* you find me?"

"I followed Gabby."

She laughed, couldn't help it. She'd expected him to lie or have some high-tech way for having found her not-publicly-listed office. But he'd told her the truth. "Awfully sneaky and underhanded for a Ranger."

His mouth curved, and the fluttering was back tenfold. He had a movie-star smile, all charm and white teeth, and while Alyssa had seen men like that in her life, she'd never, ever had that kind of smile directed at *her*.

"You must know Ranger Cooper, antithesis of all that is sneaky and underhanded. We aren't all like that."

Something about all that fluttering turned into a spiral, one that arrowed down her chest and into her belly. She felt oddly shaky, and Alyssa had long ago learned how to ward off shaky. She'd grown up in isolation as part of a criminal family. Then she'd been kidnapped for two years, locked away in little more than a bunker.

She was not a weakling. She was never scared. The scariest parts of her life were over, but something about this man sent her as off-kilter as she'd ever been.

It wasn't fear for her life or the need to fight off an attacker, but she didn't know *what* it was, and that was the scariest thing of all.

"Why are you here?" she asked, edging behind her cracked desk. She had a knife strapped to her ankle, but she'd prefer the Glock she'd shoved in the drawer when Gabby had stormed in an hour earlier.

She wouldn't use either on him, but she didn't want him to think she was going to do whatever he wanted either. He might be a Texas Ranger, but he couldn't waltz in here and get whatever he wanted. Especially if what he wanted was information about Jimenez.

"I have some questions for you, Ms. Jimenez, that's all."

"Then why is everyone trying so hard to keep you from meeting me?" Alyssa returned, sliding her hand into the drawer.

The Ranger's eyes flicked to the movement, and she didn't miss the way his hand slowly rose to the holster of *his* weapon. She paused her movement completely, but she didn't retract her hand.

"Maybe they're afraid of what I'll find out."

She raised her gaze from his gun to those shocking blue eyes. His expression was flat and grim, so very *police*. Worst of all, it sent a shiver of fear through her.

There were so very many things he could find out.

Chapter Two

Bennet didn't know what to make out of Alyssa's closed-down gas station of an office. Could anyone call this an office? It looked like nothing more than an abandoned building, except maybe she'd swept the floors a little. But the windows were grimy, the lights dim, and most of the debris of a convenience store were still scattered about.

Then there was this pretty force of a woman standing in the midst of all of it as though it were a sleek, modern office building in downtown Austin.

She wore jeans and a leather jacket over a T-shirt. The boots on her feet looked like they might weigh as much as her. Her dark hair was pulled back, and her dark eyes flashed with suspicion.

Something about her poked at him, deep in his gut. He tried to convince himself he must have dealt with her before, criminally, but he was too practical to convince himself of a lie. Whatever that poke was, it wasn't work related.

But he was here to work. To finally do something worthwhile. With no help from any outside forces.

She didn't take her hand off what he assumed to be a weapon in the drawer of her desk—though it was hidden from his view—so he kept his hand on his. Alyssa might be a friend of people he knew, but that didn't mean he trusted her.

"I guess what you find out depends on what you're looking for, Ranger…" She looked expectantly at him.

Though she was clearly suspicious, defensive even, she didn't appear nervous or scared, so he went ahead and took his hand off the butt of his weapon. He held out his hand between them. "Bennet Stevens. And I don't know why your friends are being so protective of you. All I'm after is a little information about a case I'm working on. If you have no connection to it, I'll happily walk away and not bother you again."

Nothing in her expression changed. She watched him and his outstretched hand warily. She was doing some sort of mental calculation, and Bennet figured he could wait that out and keep his hand outstretched for as long as it took.

"What kind of case?"

"A murder."

She laughed, and something in his gut tightened, a completely unwelcome sensation. She had a sexy laugh, and it was the last thing he had any business noticing.

"I can assure you I have nothing to do with any murders," Alyssa said, still ignoring his outstretched hand.

"Then what do you have to do with?" he asked, giving up on the handshake.

She cocked her head at him. "I'm pretty sure you said that if I didn't have anything to do with your case, you'd leave me alone. Well, you know where the door is."

He glanced at the door even though there was no way he was retreating anytime soon. His initial plan had been to come in here and be friendly and subtle, ease into things.

It was clear Alyssa wasn't going to respond to subtle or friendly. Which meant he had to go with the straightforward tactic, even if it ended up offending his friends.

He held up his hands, palms toward her, a clear sign he wouldn't be reaching for his weapon as he slowly withdrew two papers from his shirt's front pocket.

He unfolded the papers and handed the top one to her. "Is that you?"

It was a picture of a young girl, surrounded by five dangerous-looking men. Men who were confirmed to be part of the Jimenez drug cartel.

Bennet had no doubt the girl in the picture was Alyssa. Though she did look different as an adult, there were too many similarities. Chief among them the stony expression on her face.

She looked at the picture for an abnormally long time in utter silence.

"Ms. Jimenez?"

She looked up at him, and there wasn't just stony stoicism or cynicism in her expression anymore, there was something a lot closer to hatred. She dropped the picture on her ramshackle desk.

"I really doubt I need to answer that question since you're here. You've decided it's me whether I confirm it or not. You clearly know who those men are, decided I'm connected to them. I doubt you'll believe me, but let me head you off at the pass. I have not contacted anyone with the last name Jimenez since I was *kidnapped* at the age of twenty."

He wouldn't let that soften him. "Then I guess it's fitting that the case I'm looking into is sixteen years old."

Confusion drew her eyebrows together. "You want to question me about a crime that happened when I was eight?"

"Yes."

She made a scoffing noise disguised as a laugh. "All right, Ranger Hotshot. Hit me."

"Sixteen years ago, a Jane Doe was found murdered. She's never been identified, but I found some similarities between her case and a case connected to the Jimenez family. *Your* family. I'd like to bring some closure to this cold case, and I think you can help."

"I was eight. Whatever my brothers were doing, I had no part in."

"Brothers?"

She didn't move, didn't say anything, but Bennet nearly smiled. She'd slipped up and given him more information than he'd had. He'd known Alyssa was connected, but he hadn't known how close.

Yeah, she was going to be exactly what he needed. "I'd like you to look at the picture of the Jane Doe and let me know if you remember ever seeing her with your *brothers*. It's not an incredibly graphic picture, but it can be disconcerting for some people to view pictures of dead bodies."

Alyssa rolled her eyes and snatched up the picture. "I work as a bounty hunter. I think I can stand the sight of a…" But she trailed off and paled. She sank into the folding chair so hard it broke and she fell to the ground.

Bennet was at her side not quite in time to keep her ass from hitting the floor. "Are you okay?"

She was shaking, seemed not to have noticed she'd broken a chair and was sitting in its debris, the picture fisted in her hand.

"Alyssa?"

When she finally brought her gaze to his, those brown eyes were wide and wet and she was clearly in shock.

"Where'd you get this?" she demanded in a whisper, her hands shaking. Hell, her whole body was shaking. Her brown eyes bored into his. "This is a lie. This has to be a lie." Her voice cracked.

"You know her?" he asked, gently rubbing a hand

up and down her forearm, trying to offer *something* to help her stop shaking so hard.

Alyssa looked back down at the picture that shook in her hands. "That's my mother."

THE TEARS WERE sharp and burning, but Alyssa did everything she could to keep them from falling. She forced herself to look away from the picture and shoved it back at the Texas Ranger, whatever his name was.

It wasn't true. It couldn't be true. Her mother had *left* her. She'd been seduced away by some rival of her father's. *That* was the story.

Not murder.

It didn't make sense. None of it made any sense. She tried to get ahold of her labored breathing, but no matter how much she told herself to breathe slowly in and out, she could only gasp and pant, that picture of her mother's lifeless face seared into her brain forever.

Murder.

She realized the Ranger had stopped rubbing her arm in that oddly comforting gesture and instead curled long, strong fingers around both her elbows.

"Come on," he said gently, pulling her to her feet.

Since the debris of the rickety chair that had broken underneath her weight was starting to dig into her butt, she let him do it. Once she was standing somewhere close to steady on her feet, he didn't release her. No, that strong grip stayed right where it was on her elbows.

It was centering somehow, that firm, warm pressure. A reminder she existed in the here and now, not in one of the different prisons her life had been.

She blinked up at the Texas Ranger holding her steady. There was something like compassion in his blue eyes, maybe even regret. His full lips were downturned, slight grooves bracketing his mouth.

He was something like pretty, and she'd rather have those cheekbones and that square jaw burned into her brain than the image of her dead mother.

"If I'd had any idea, Alyssa…" he said, his voice gravel and his tone overly familiar.

She pulled herself out of his grasp, pulled into herself, like she'd learned how to do time and time again as the inconsequential daughter of a criminal, as a useless kidnapping victim.

She'd spent the last two years trying to build a life for herself where she might matter, where she might do some *good*.

This moment forced her back into all the ways she'd never mattered. What other lies she'd accepted as truth might be waiting for her?

She closed her eyes against the onslaught of pain. And fear.

"My brothers didn't murder my mother, Ranger Stevens," Alyssa managed, though her voice was rusty. "I know they're not exactly heroes, but they never would have killed my mother."

"Okay." He was quiet for a few humming seconds. "Maybe you'd like to help me find out who did."

She didn't move, didn't emote. She'd worked with law enforcement before, but she was careful about it. They usually didn't know her name or her friends. They definitely didn't know her connection to the Jimenez family.

This man knew all of that and had to look like Superman in a cowboy hat on top of it. The last thing she should consider was working with him.

Except her mother was dead. Murdered. A Jane Doe for well over a decade, and as much as she couldn't believe her brothers had anything to do with her mother's murder—*murder*—she couldn't believe they didn't know. There was no way Miranda Jimenez had stayed a Jane Doe without her family purposefully making sure she did.

Alyssa swallowed. Making sure her mother had stayed a Jane Doe, all the while making sure Alyssa didn't know about it. Her brothers had always claimed they were protecting her by keeping things from her, and it was hard to doubt. They *had* meant well. If they hadn't, she'd have been dead or auctioned off to some faithful servant of her father's before she'd ever been kidnapped.

Ranger Stevens released her, and she felt cold without that warm, sturdy grip. Cold and alone. *Well, that's what you are. What you'll always have to be.*

"Take some time. Come to grips with this new information, and when you're ready to work with me, give me a call." He pulled his wallet out of his back pocket and handed her a card from it.

She took the card. That big star emblem of the Rangers seemed to stare at her. It looked so official, so *heroic*, that symbol. Right next to it, his name, *Bennet E. Stevens. Ranger.*

She glanced back up at him, and was more than a little irritated she saw kindness in his expression. She didn't want kindness or compassion. She didn't know what to do with those things, and she already got them in spades from Gabby and Natalie and even to an extent from their law enforcement significant others.

Everyone felt sorry for Alyssa Jimenez, but no one knew who she really was. Except this man.

"Do you have a phone number I can reach you at?" he prompted when she didn't say anything.

She didn't want to give him her number. She didn't want to give him anything. She wanted to rewind the last half hour and go with Gabby to the hospital. She would have avoided this whole thing.

Not forever, though. She was too practical to think it would have lasted forever.

"Fine," she muttered, because, as much as she knew she'd end up working with this guy, the promise of solving her mother's murder was too great, too important, and she didn't want to give him too much leverage. She'd make him think she was reticent, doing *him* a favor when she finally agreed.

She grabbed a pen and scrap of paper from her

desk and scrawled her number on it. He took it, sliding it into his pocket along with the pictures he'd retrieved. She'd wanted to keep them, but she had to keep it cool. She'd get them eventually.

"I'll be in touch, Alyssa," he said with a tip of his hat. He paused for a second, hesitating. "I am sorry for your loss," he said gravely, before turning and exiting her office.

She let out a shaky sigh. The worst thing was believing that kind of crap. Why would he be sorry? He didn't know her or her mother. It was a lame, placating statement.

It soothed somehow, idiot that she was. She shook her head and collected her belongings. She'd stop by the hospital to check on Natalie and Gabby, and then she'd go home and try to sleep. She'd give it a day, maybe two, then she'd call Ranger Too-Hot-For-Her-Own-Good.

She locked up and exited out the back, pulling her helmet on before starting her motorcycle. It was her most expensive possession, and she treated it like a baby. Nothing in the world gave her the freedom that motorcycle did.

She rode out of the alley and onto the street that would lead her to the highway and the hospital. Within two minutes, she knew she was being followed.

Her first inclination was that it was Ranger Stevens keeping tabs on her, but the jacked-up piece-of-crap car following her was no Texas Ranger vehicle.

She scowled and narrowed her eyes. Of course, anyone could be following her, but after the Ranger's visit and information, Alyssa had the sneaking suspicion it was all related.

Maybe her brothers had ignored her existence since she'd been kidnapped and then released, but that didn't mean they couldn't find her if they wanted to.

If they were after her now, they wouldn't give up until they got her. But that didn't mean she had to go down easy. Certainly not after they'd abandoned her.

She took a sharp turn onto a side street, then weaved in and out of traffic the way the car couldn't. She took a few more sharp turns, earning honks and angry middle fingers from other drivers, but eventually she found herself in a dark, small alley. She killed her engine and stood there straddling her bike, breathing heavily.

Did her brothers know Ranger Stevens was investigating their mother's death? Did they have something to hide?

She squeezed her eyes shut, finding her even breathing. They couldn't have killed their mother. They couldn't have. Alyssa couldn't bring herself to believe it.

Her phone rang and she swore, expecting it to be news about Natalie's baby. Instead, it was a number she didn't recognize. Her brothers?

She hit Accept cautiously, and adopted her best take-no-crap tone. "What?"

"You're being tailed."

She scowled at Ranger Steven's voice. "I'm well aware. I lost them."

"Yeah, well, I'm tailing them now."

"Idiot," she muttered. How had this man stepped into her life for fifteen minutes and scrambled everything up?

"What?" Ranger Stevens spluttered.

Alyssa had to think fast. To move. Oh, damn the man for getting in the way of things. "Listen, I'm coming back out. I want you to let them follow me. And when they take me, I need you to not get in the way." Her brothers had never come for her, and she'd stopped expecting them, but if they were coming for her now…she was ready.

As long as she could get rid of the Texas Ranger trying to protect her.

Chapter Three

Bennet wanted to argue, but he had to keep too much of his attention on following the men who'd been following Alyssa to try to outtalk this girl.

Let them take her? "Are you crazy?"

"We both know it's someone from my family, or sent by them anyway. If I let them take me, I get information."

"And end up like your mother." Which was probably too blunt when she'd only just found out about her mother, but he couldn't keep compassion in place when she was talking about getting herself abducted.

He heard a motorcycle engine roar past him, and swore when Alyssa waved at him.

He tossed his phone into the passenger seat and followed. It was reckless and possibly stupid not to call for backup. But while Captain Dean had given him the go-ahead to take on this case, Bennet wasn't ready to bring in other people yet. He needed more information. He needed to know what he was dealing with.

The fact of the matter was he had no idea what he was dealing with when it came to Alyssa Jimenez.

She cut in front of the car that had originally been following her. He watched the streetlights streak across her quickly moving form, and she waved at those guys too.

She *was* crazy.

While Bennet had been worried in the beginning that the tail's goal had been to hurt Alyssa, it was clear they were after something else. If they wanted to hurt her, they could run her off the road and drive away. No one would know the difference except him, and Bennet didn't think they knew *they* had a tail.

It was clear they wanted Alyssa. Whole. She had wanted him to let them take her, so it seemed she knew she wasn't in imminent danger from these people, as well.

Was she working with them? Was he the fool here?

Except when she finally quit driving, he could only stare from his place farther down the street. She'd led them to the public parking of the Texas Rangers headquarters.

What on earth was this woman up to?

She parked in the middle of the mostly empty parking lot—employees parked in the back and public visitors rarely arrived at night. The car that had been following her stopped at the parking lot entrance. Clearly her followers didn't know what to do with this.

Bennet made a turn, keeping the parking lot in view from his rearview window. When the car didn't follow, the occupants instead kept their attention on Alyssa, he knew they hadn't seen him following them.

He made a quick sharp turn into the back lot and then drove along the building, parking as close as he could to where Alyssa was without being seen. He got out of his car and unholstered his weapon. He crept along the building, keeping himself in the shadows, watching as the car still idled in the entrance while Alyssa sat defiantly on her motorcycle in the middle of the parking lot, parking lights haloing her.

That uncomfortable thing from before tightened in his gut at the way the light glinted off her dark hair when she pulled off her helmet. Something a little lower than his gut reacted far too much at the "screw you" in the curve of her mouth. She looked like some fierce warrior, some underground-gang queen. He should not be attracted to that even for a second.

Apparently some parts of his anatomy weren't as interested in law and order as his brain was.

"What are you guys? Chicken?" Alyssa called out.

Bennet nearly groaned. She would have to be the kind of woman who'd provoke them.

"How about this—you send a message to my brothers. You tell them if they want me, they can come get me themselves. No cut-rate, brainless thug is going to take me anywhere I don't want to go."

The engine revved, and Bennet moved closer. He

wasn't going to let these men take his only lead on this case. Even if she was trying to get herself killed.

But in the end, the car merely backed out and screeched away.

Leaving him and Alyssa in a mostly empty parking lot.

She turned to face him as if she'd known he was there all along. "I bet that got their attention, huh?" she said. She didn't walk toward him, so he walked to her.

"Yes. How smart. Piss off your criminal brothers you claim to have nothing to do with so they come after you."

"Yes, exactly."

"I thought you wanted me to let them take you." Which he never would have done.

"I was going to, but then I saw what cut-rate weaklings they sent after me. Afraid of a little Texas Ranger parking lot." She made a scoffing sound. "The only way to really get some answers is to get inside again, but guys like that? Dopes with guns? Yeah, I'm not risking my life with them. My brothers can come get me themselves if it's that important to them."

"You're not going back inside that family."

She raised an eyebrow at him. "Since when did you become my keeper?"

"Since I'm the reason you think you need to go back there. We'll investigate this from the outside. You don't need to be on the inside." He'd sacrifice a lot to actually accomplish something, but not someone else's life.

"Shows what you know. Not a damn thing. I've been gone a long time, but I still know how the Jimenez family works. I can get the answers we need."

"*We* need?"

She looked at her motorcycle, helmet still dangling from her fingertips. He'd watched her shake and tremble apart after seeing her mother's picture, but she was nothing but strength and certainty now.

Again, Bennet couldn't help but wonder if he was the sucker here, if he was being pulled into something that would end up making a fool out of him. But he'd come too far to back out. Gotten the okay on this case, gotten to Alyssa. He had to keep moving forward.

"My brothers didn't murder our mom," she said, raising her gaze to his. Strong and sure. "I know they didn't. I'm going to prove it. To you. And when you find out who really did it, you can bring them to justice."

Her voice shook at the end, though her shoulders-back, chin-up stance didn't change.

He couldn't trust her. She was related to one of the biggest drug cartels in the state. And while Gabby and Natalie had befriended her, and Vaughn thought she hadn't had contact with her brothers in years, this felt awfully coincidental.

She must have seen the direction of his thoughts.

"You don't have to trust me, Ranger Stevens. You just have to stay out of my way."

"I'm afraid I can't do that." No matter what it took, he had knocked over whatever domino was creating these events. He was part of it, and whether he trusted her or not, he had some responsibility for bringing her into this.

"They must have my office bugged," Alyssa said, scowling. "The timing is too coincidental, too weird. It's been two years since the kidnapping rescue, and they've left me alone. They had to have heard you questioning me. So, they know. You have to stay out of my way so we can know what's *really* going on."

"How can you think they had nothing to do with it if they're stepping in now when they supposedly know what I'm after?"

"They didn't kill our mother, but cartel business is tricky. Complicated. Their never identifying her when she was Jane Doe, it could be purposeful or they feel like they can't now or… I don't know, but I have to find out. I'm going in. You can't stop me, and God knows you can't stop them."

He didn't agree with that. He could put a security detail on her, keep her safe and away from her brothers for the foreseeable future. Even if the Rangers pulled support, he had enough of his own money to make it so.

But it'd be awfully hard to make it so when she was so determined, and it'd make it harder to get the information he needed. It would make it almost impossible to solve this case.

He studied her, looking at him so defiantly, as if she was the one in charge here. As if she could stand up to him, toe-to-toe, over and over again. Some odd thing shuddered through him, a gut feeling he didn't want to pay attention to.

He'd made his decision, so there was only one way to settle this. "If you're going in, then I'm going in with you."

AND THIS TEXAS Ranger thought *she* was crazy.

"You think you're going to come with me. You think in *any* world my brothers would allow a Texas Ranger into their home or office or whatever without, oh, say killing you and making sure no one ever found out about it?"

"Except you."

Unfortunately, he had a point. Also unfortunately, her last name might keep her safe for the most part when it came to the Jimenez family, but she knew without a shadow of a doubt, if she outright betrayed her family, she'd be killed.

Like your mother.

She couldn't get over it, so she just kept pushing the reality out of her mind as much as she could. Still, it lingered in whispers. *Murdered. Murdered. Murdered.* How on earth could Mom have been murdered? It didn't make any sense.

Except she left. Betrayed your father. Maybe it makes all the sense in the world.

She couldn't. She just couldn't. She couldn't focus on possibility. She had to focus on truth.

"I can handle this," Ranger Stevens said resolutely.

"No. You can handle being a Texas Ranger. You can handle being a cop. You can't handle being inside a drug cartel. Even if they let you, you'd want to arrest everyone. And trust me, that wouldn't go well for you."

"They didn't hurt you. They ran away."

"Of course they didn't hurt me. Even if I'm not involved in the business, I'm the daughter of a cartel kingpin. I'm the sister of the people who run it. They hurt me, they're dead. It's a matter of honor, but that doesn't mean that protection extends to you." Or to her, if she betrayed Jimenez.

"So we'll have to find a way for them to think it's a matter of honor not to kill me."

"How on earth do you suggest we do that?"

"I have a few ideas, but I'm not discussing them here in this parking lot." He gestured toward the Texas Rangers building.

Alyssa laughed. "I'm not going in there. My brothers are going to think I'm working with you on a lot more than Mom's..." she cleared her throat of the lump "...murder."

"You know it isn't just me at stake here. Natalie

and Gabby. Their families. They're a part of your life, and now—"

She took a threatening step toward him—or it might have been threatening, if he wasn't about six inches taller than her and twice as wide. "You don't think I know that? You don't think I have made my life very separate so they would never get pulled into this if I had to be?"

"I don't know you at all, Alyssa. I don't know what your plans are."

"My plan is to live a normal life. That's all I want." She realized, too late, she'd yelled it, shaking all over again. Normal had seemed almost within reach lately, and then this Texas Ranger had walked into her office and everything had changed.

She was Alyssa Jimenez again. Not bounty hunter and friend, not even kidnapping victim, or the inconsequential relative of very consequential people. She was in danger and in trouble, and she couldn't do anything about it.

He reached out, and she hated that something like a simple touch on her arm could just *soothe*. She'd never understood it, but Gabby would hug her back in that bunker, and even out here in the open, and everything would feel okay. This guy, this stranger of a Texas Ranger, touched her, and it felt like she could handle whatever came if he was touching her.

It was insanity.

"If they bugged your office, it's likely they've bugged your house."

Alyssa thought of her little apartment above Gabby and Jaime's garage. Was it bugged? Was the whole house bugged? Had she brought all of her family's problems into the house they'd been kind enough to open up to her?

Guilt swamped her, pain. Tears threatened, but she wouldn't be that weak. She'd fix this. She had to fix this.

"Come home with me."

She jerked her head up to look at Ranger Stevens and carefully pulled herself out of his grasp. Everything in her rebelled at the idea of going home with him. His house. His life. Him.

"I have a big house. Multiple rooms. You can have your own bathroom, your own space. We can get some sleep, and in the morning we can talk knowing that no one has bugged my place."

"They know who you are now. If they bugged my place, they know your name. They know what you're after."

He seemed to consider that with more weight than she thought he would. "All right. I have somewhere else we can go. It might require a little bending of the truth."

Alyssa frowned at him. "What kind of bending of the truth?"

"We'll just need to pretend this isn't related to my job. That you're not so much a professional acquaintance but a, ah, personal one."

"Where the hell are you taking me?" she demanded, touching her bike to remind herself she was free. He couldn't take her anywhere unless she agreed.

And if you go home, would you be putting Gabby and Jaime in jeopardy?

"My parents have a guesthouse. I use it on occasion when necessary. I can say I'm having my house painted or remodeled or something and they'll believe it, if they're even home. But if I'm bringing you with me, they're going to need to think…" He cleared his throat.

Alyssa's mouth went slack as it dawned on her what he was suggesting. "You want me to pretend to be involved with you like…sleeping-over involved?" Her voice squeaked and her entire face heated. Her whole body heated. She'd never been sleeping-over involved with anyone, and she was pretty sure that was a really lame way of putting it, but she didn't know how else to say it.

She didn't know how to wrap her head around what he was suggesting.

"My parents aren't invasive exactly. Actually, they're incredibly invasive, but like I said, it's unlikely they're there. They have some of the best security in Austin, so we'll be safe, or at least forewarned. Should one of the staff mention I had a woman over, then they'll assume it's personal and we'll just go with it."

"Your parents have a guesthouse and staff?"

"Your father runs a drug cartel?" he returned in the same put-off tone.

She wanted to laugh even though it wasn't funny in the least little bit. "No one's going to believe I'm involved with...*you*."

Something in his expression changed, a softening followed by an all-too-charming smile that had her heart beating hard against her chest.

"Am I that hideous?" he asked, clearly knowing full well he was *not*.

"You know what I mean. I look like a street urchin," she said, waving a hand down her front. "You look like..." She waved her hand ineffectually at him.

He cocked his head. "I look like what?" he asked, and there was something a little darker in his tone. Dangerous. But cops weren't dangerous. Not like that.

"I don't know," she muttered, knowing she had to be blushing so profusely even the bad lighting couldn't hide it. "A guy who has servants and guesthouses and crap."

"They'll believe it because there's no reason not to. Street-urchin chic or no, my parents wouldn't doubt me. They might assume I'm trying to give them an aneurism, but they won't suspect anything."

Alyssa looked at her bike. She could hop on, flip him off and zoom away. Zoom away from everything she'd built in the past two years, zoom away from everything that had held her prisoner for the first twenty-two.

But she hadn't left Austin on her release from her kidnapper, and she had people to protect now. She couldn't leave Gabby and Natalie in the middle of this, even if they were both married to men or living with men who would try to protect them.

She studied Ranger Stevens and knew she had to make a choice. Fight, and trust this man. Or run, and ruin them all.

It wasn't a hard choice in the slightest. "All right. I'll go."

Chapter Four

Bennet drove from the Texas Ranger offices to his parents' sprawling estate outside Austin. It wasn't the first time he'd been self-conscious about his parents' wealth. Most of the cops and Rangers he knew were not the sons and daughters of the Texas elite.

Nevertheless, this was the life he'd been born into, and Alyssa hadn't been born into a much different one. Just on opposite sides of the law, but if her father was the Jimenez kingpin, then she'd had her share of wealth.

She followed him, the roar of her motorcycle cutting through the quiet of the wealthy neighborhood enough to make him wince. There would be phone calls. There would be a lot of things. But the most important thing was they were going somewhere that couldn't have been infiltrated.

He drove up the sprawling drive after entering the code for the gate and hoped against hope his father was in DC and his mother was at a function or, well, anywhere but here. Because while they might ignore his presence, maybe, they would never ignore the presence of the motorcycle.

Parking at the top of the drive, he got out of his running car and punched the code into the garage door so it opened.

"*This* is a guesthouse?" Alyssa called out over the sound of her motorcycle.

Bennet nodded as the garage door went up. He walked back to his car and motioned for her to park inside the garage. Maybe if the evidence was hidden, and it was late enough, it was possible no one would notice the disturbance. A man could dream.

Alyssa walked her motorcycle into the garage and killed the engine. She pulled off her helmet. It seemed no matter how often her hair tumbled out like that, his idiotic body had a reaction. He really needed to get a handle on that.

"Follow me," he said, probably too tersely. But he felt terse and uncomfortable. He felt a lot of things he didn't want to think about.

He slid the key he always kept on his ring into the lock of the door from the garage to the mudroom. He didn't look back to see how she reacted to the rather ostentatious guesthouse as they walked through it. It wasn't his.

He led her into the living room. "Feel free to use anything in the house. The fridge probably won't be stocked, but the pantry is. The staff keeps everything clean and fresh for visitors, so—"

"You keep saying 'staff,' but I have a feeling what you mean is servants."

He gave her a doleful look. "I'll show you to a bedroom and bathroom you can use. I suggest we get some sleep and reevaluate in the morning."

"Reevaluate what?"

"How we're going to handle getting me into see your brothers with you."

"There's no way. There's *no* way. They'll kill you on sight knowing you're a Texas Ranger. They have all this time while we're 'reevaluating' to plan to kill you and make it look like an accident, make you just disappear." She snapped her fingers. "It will be suicide. I don't think you get that."

"I told you I had some ideas."

"Like what?"

"Like what we're doing right here."

She threw her arms up in the air, clearly frustrated with him. "What are we doing right here?

"If your brothers think that we..." He cleared his throat, uncomfortable with his own idea, with telling it to her, with *enacting* it. But it made sense. It was the only thing that made sense. No matter how much he didn't want to do it. "If your brothers think we are romantically involved, there's a chance they wouldn't touch me. If I were important to you."

Alyssa blinked at him for a full minute. "First of all," she said eventually, "even if that was remotely true, if they have my office bugged, they know we just met. It was part of that conversation."

"We'll say it was a lure."

"You can't be this stupid. You can't be."

That offhanded insult poked at a million things he'd never admit to. "I assure you, Ms. Jimenez, I know what I'm doing," he said, crossing his arms over his chest and giving her a look that had intimidated drug dealers and rapists and even murderers.

Alyssa rolled her eyes. "Spare me the 'Ms. Jimenez' crap. It makes far more sense for me to go there on my own and handle things my own way. You can trust me when I say I want to get to the bottom of my mother's murder more than you do. I have no reason not to bring you whatever information I find so my mother's murderer can be brought to justice."

"I think you're bright enough to realize all of this is so much more than a murder case. The things your brothers are involved in aren't that easy. It's not something I can trust a civilian to go into and bring me back the information I need to prosecute. I need to go in there with you. I need to investigate this myself."

She shook her head in disgust, but she didn't argue further. Which was a plus.

"How far are you willing to go?" she demanded.

"As far as I need to. This case is my number one priority. I won't rest until it's solved."

She sighed while looking around the living room. "I can't sit anywhere in here. I'll stain all this white just by looking at it."

He rolled his eyes and took her by the elbow, leading her to a chair. It *was* white, and it was very possible she'd get motorcycle grease or something on it, but it would be taken care of. Stains in the Stevens world were always taken care of.

He pushed her into the chair. She sat with an audible thump. "What about this? You tell them I'm a double agent. That I want to be a dirty cop."

"They wouldn't believe that."

"Why not?"

"Because you are the antithesis of a dirty cop. You look like Superman had a baby with Captain America and every other do-gooder superhero to ever exist. No one would believe you want to be a dirty cop."

"Have you ever had any contact with a dirty cop?"

"Well, no."

He took a seat on the couch, leaning forward and resting his elbows on his knees. He never took his eyes off her—this was too important. "It has nothing to do with what you look like and everything to do with how desperate you are. How powerful you want to feel. Cops go dirty because… Well, there are a lot of reasons, but it's not about how you look or where you're from. It's about ego, among other things."

"Okay, it's about ego, which I'll give you you've got, but that doesn't mean they're going to believe any of it."

"It doesn't mean they won't."

"You're not going to give up on this, are you?"

"We can do it the easy way or the hard way. The

easy way is where you work with me. The hard way is where you work against me. Either way, I'm doing it."

She sighed gustily, but he could see in the set of her shoulders she was relenting. Giving in. One way or another, she was going to give in.

"Fine. But we're not doing it your way. If we're doing it together, when it comes to my brothers, we do it *my* way. I tell them I'm using you to get information. I don't know if they'll buy it hook, line and sinker, but it's better than all your ideas."

"Gee, thank you."

"I'm afraid you're going to have to leave your ego at the door, Mr. Texas Ranger."

"I'll see what I can do."

Alyssa rubbed her temples. She had to be exhausted and stressed and emotionally wrung out from the things she'd found out today.

"Let's go to bed. We'll work out the details in the morning."

She sighed and pushed herself out of the chair. "Fine. Lead me to my castle."

"You're awfully melodramatic for a street urchin."

"I'm not the one living in this place."

"I don't live in this place," he muttered, standing, as well.

"You also don't live in an apartment above a garage."

"Is that where you live?" Which was neither here nor there, knowing where she lived or anything about her current life. All that mattered was her connection to the Jimenez family.

"Yes. I live in an apartment above the garage of my friends' house. My friends who are now in danger because of me, because of this." She let out a long sigh and faced him, her expression grave, her eyes reflecting some of the fear she'd kept impressively hidden thus far. "I need them safe, Ranger Stevens."

"I may not know Gabby very well, but I've worked with Jaime on occasion, and Vaughn has been my partner for a long time. I care about your friends. They're *my* friends, too. Nothing's going to happen to them."

"My, you are a confident one."

But no matter how sarcastically she'd said it, he could see a slight relaxation in her. His confidence gave her comfort. "Confidence is everything."

"Except when you have nothing."

Bennet didn't know what to say to that, so he led her down a hallway to the bedrooms. The farthest one from his. It would be the best room for her, not just for keeping her far away from him. He wasn't that weak to need a barrier, or so he'd tell himself.

"That door back there leads to a private bathroom. Feel free to use it and anything in it. I'll see you in the morning."

"Hey, have you heard anything from Vaughn about Nat?"

Bennet looked down at his phone. "I don't have any messages."

"I don't know what to tell them. They'll expect me to visit, and…" She shook her head, looking young and vulnerable for the first time since she'd seen the picture of her mother.

He wanted to help. He wanted to soothe. Which was just his *nature*. He was a guy who wanted to help. It had nothing to do with soft brown eyes and a pretty mouth.

"You're a bounty hunter, right? Well, an un-authorized and illegal one, anyway."

She frowned at him. "Yes. I have my reasons."

"Criminals always do." But he grinned, hoping the joke, the teasing, would lighten her up, take that vulnerable cast of her mouth away. "Tell them you had an important case, and you'll be back as soon as possible. You're not going back to your place, so it's not like they'll have any reason to believe you're in town."

"I don't like lying to them."

"It's not my favorite either, but—"

"I know. It'll keep them safe, and that is the most important thing to me."

"It's important to me, too. Never doubt that."

She nodded, hugging herself and looking around the room. "You know this kind of insane show of wealth is usually the sign of a small dick, right?"

He choked on his own spit. That had not been at all what he'd expected her to say, but from her grin he could tell that's exactly why she'd said it.

"I suppose that's something you'd have to take

up with my father, since this is neither my show of wealth, nor is that a complaint I've ever received."

Two twin blotches of pink showed up on her cheeks, and Bennet knew it was time to close the door and walk away before there were any more jokes about...that.

"Are you sure your parents won't get wind of this?"

"Unless it furthers their political agenda, my parents won't be sticking their nose anywhere near it. They'll stay out of it and safe."

"Political agenda?"

"Oh, didn't you put it together?" he asked casually, because he knew much like her small-dick comment had caught *him* off guard, this little tidbit would catch *her* off guard.

"Put what together?"

"My father is Gary L. Stevens, US senator and former presidential candidate. My mother is Lynette Stevens, pioneer lawyer and Texas state senator. You may have heard of them."

She stared slack-jawed at him, and he couldn't ignore the pleasure he got out of leaving her in shock. So he flashed a grin, his politicians' son grin.

"Good night, Alyssa."

And Bennet left her room, closing the door behind him.

ALYSSA TOSSED AND TURNED. Between trying to come to full grips with the fact that Bennet Stevens was the son of two wealthy and influential politicians, and Gabby being mad about her taking a job before coming to see the baby, she couldn't get her mind to stop running in circles.

She hated when someone was mad at her and had every right to be. She hated disappointing Gabby and Nat. But this was keeping them safe, and she had to remember that.

And more than all of that, the thing she kept trying to pretend wasn't true.

Her mother had been murdered. She knew Ranger Stevens suspected her brothers. No matter what horrible things they were capable of, though—and they were enormously capable—Alyssa rejected the idea they could be behind the murder of her mother. *Their* mother.

Maybe she could see it if her father was still in his right mind, but he had succumbed to some kind of dementia before she'd even been kidnapped. He was nothing but a titular figure now, one her brothers kept as a weapon of their own.

Once it was finally a reasonable hour to get up, Alyssa crawled out of the too-comfortable bed and looked at herself in the gigantic mirror. She looked like a bedraggled sewer animal in the midst of all this pristine white.

It was such a glaring contrast. Though she'd grown up surrounded by a certain amount of wealth, it had all been the dark-and-dirty kind. She'd lived in a sketchy guarded-to-the-hilt home for most of her life, and then been kidnapped into a glorified bunker.

But what did contrasts matter when she was simply out for the truth? She tiptoed down the hallway, wondering where Ranger Stevens had secreted himself off to last night. What would he look like sleep-rumpled in one of those big white beds?

She was seriously losing it. Clearly she needed something to eat to clear her head. She headed for the kitchen, but stopped short at the entrance when she saw Ranger Stevens was already sitting there in a little breakfast nook surrounded by windows.

"Good morning," he offered, as if it wasn't five in the morning and as if this wasn't weird as all get out.

"Morning," she replied.

On the glossy black table in front of him, he had a laptop open. He was wearing sweatpants and a T-shirt, and while the button-down shirt he'd been wearing last night hadn't exactly hidden the fact this man was no pencil pusher, this was a whole other experience.

He had muscles. Actual biceps. Whether it was on purpose or not, the sleeves of his T-shirt hugged them perfectly and made her realize, again, how unbearably hot this man was. And how unbearably unfair that was.

"There's coffee already brewed. Mugs are in the cabinet above it. As for breakfast, feel free to poke around and find what you'd like."

"Not much of a breakfast eater," she lied. She

didn't know why she lied. She just felt off-kilter and weird and didn't want to be here.

"I'd try to eat something. Got a lot of work to do today."

"Don't you have to go to, like, actual work?"

"My actual work is investigating this case."

"If my brothers get ahold of you and you don't report for work, what's going to happen then?"

He looked at her over his laptop with that hard, implacable Texas Ranger look she thought maybe he practiced in the mirror. Because it was effective, both in shutting her up and making those weird lower-belly flutters intensify.

"I'll handle my work responsibilities," he said, his voice deep and certain.

Alyssa rolled her eyes in an effort to appear wholly unaffected. She walked over to the coffeepot. She didn't drink coffee, but she figured she might as well start. That's what adults did after all. They drank coffee and handled their work responsibilities.

"Sugar is right next to the pot. No cream, but milk is in the fridge."

"I drink it black," she lied. She tried to take a sophisticated sip, but ended up burning her tongue and grimacing at the horrible, horrible taste.

"You take it black, huh?" And there was that dangerous curve to his mouth, humor and something like intent all curled into it. She wanted to trace it with her fingers.

So, she scowled instead. "Let's worry less about

how I take my coffee and more about what we're going to do."

"First things first, we're going to go back to your office and check for a bug. We need to know exactly what your brothers know about me and what I'm looking for."

She wasn't in love with him deciding what they were going to do without at least a conversation, but unfortunately he was right. They needed to know for sure what was going on.

"Once we've figured that out, we'll move on to trying to lure your brothers out."

"I'm guessing my leading their cronies to Texas Rangers headquarters and yelling probably did it."

"Probably, but we need to make sure. We also need to make sure it seems like we don't want to be caught."

She studied him then because there was something not quite right about all this.

"This is official Ranger business, right?"

He focused on the computer. "What do you mean 'official'?"

"This isn't on the up-and-up, is it?"

His mouth firmed and his jaw went hard and uncompromising. He was so damn hot, and she kind of wanted to lick him. She didn't know what to do with that. She'd never wanted to lick anyone before.

"I've been okayed to investigate this case," he ground out. "It's possible we'll have to do some things that aren't entirely by the book. I might not tell my superiors every single thing I'm doing, but this is one of those cases where you have to bend the rules a little bit."

"Doesn't bending the rules invalidate the investigation?"

"Depends on the situation. Do you want to find the answers to your mother's murder or not?"

Which she supposed was all that really mattered. She wanted to find the answers to her mother's murder. Everything else was secondary. "Okay. Well, let's go, then."

His mouth quirked, his hard, uncompromising expression softening. "Aren't you going to finish your coffee?"

She glanced at the mug, and she knew he was testing her. Teasing her maybe. She fluttered her eyelashes at him. "You make shitty coffee."

He barked out a laugh, and she was all too pleased he was laughing at something she'd said. All too pleased he would tease her. Pay attention to her in any way.

It was stupid to be into him. So she'd ignore that part of herself right now. Ignore the flutters and the being pleased.

A door opened somewhere, and Bennet visibly cringed when a voice rang out.

"Bennet? Are you here?"

It was a woman's voice. Did he have a girlfriend? Something ugly bloomed in her chest, but Bennet offered some sort of half grimace, half smile. "Well, Alyssa, let's see what kind of actress you are."

He pushed away from the table, and an older woman entered the room. He held out his arms.

"Mother. How are you?"

"Surprised to find you here." She brushed her lips across the air next to Bennet's cheek.

Alyssa pushed herself into the little corner of the countertop, but Bennet wasn't going to let her be ignored. He turned his mother to face her.

"Allow me to introduce you to someone," he said easily, charmingly, clearly a very good actor. The woman's blue gaze landed on Alyssa.

"This is Alyssa… Clark," Bennet offered. "Alyssa, this is my mother, Lynette Stevens."

"Alyssa Clark," Mrs. Stevens repeated blandly.

Alyssa didn't have to be a mind reader to know Mrs. Stevens did not approve. She might have squirmed if it didn't piss her off a little. Sure, she looked like a drowned sewer rat and was the daughter of a drug kingpin rather than Texas royalty, but she wasn't a bad person. Exactly.

Alyssa smiled as sweetly as she could manage. "It's so good to meet you, Ms. Stevens. I've heard *so* much about you," she said, adopting her most cultured, overly upper-class Texas drawl.

Mrs. Bennet's expression didn't change, but Alyssa was adept at reading the cold fury of people. And Mrs. Stevens had some cold fury going on in there.

"I didn't realize you were seeing anyone at the moment, Bennet," Mrs. Stevens murmured, the fury of her gaze never leaving Alyssa.

"I don't tell you everything, as you well know."

"Yes, well. I just came by to see what all the noise complaints were about. If I'd known you were busy, I wouldn't have bothered you."

"It was no bother, but I do have to get ready for work."

"And what's Ms. Clark going to do while you work?"

"Oh, I have my own work to do," Alyssa said. She smiled as blandly and coldly as Bennet's mother.

"Yes, well. I'll leave you both alone then. Try to avoid any more noise disturbances if you please, and if you're around this evening, bring your young lady to dinner at the main house."

"I'll see if our schedules can accommodate it and let Kinsey know," Bennet replied, and Alyssa had not seen this side of him. Cool and blank, a false mask of charm over everything. This was not Ranger Stevens, and she didn't think it was Bennet either.

"Wonderful. I hope to see you then." She gave Alyssa one last glance and then swept out of the kitchen as quickly as she'd appeared.

Alyssa looked curiously at Bennet. "That's how you talk to your mother?"

"I'm afraid so."

"Why did she hate me so much?"

"You're not on her approved list of women I'm allowed to see."

"She doesn't have a list."

Bennet raised an eyebrow. "It's laminated."

Alyssa laughed, even though she had a terrible feeling he wasn't joking. "So, she wants you to get married and have lots of little perfect Superman babies?"

"It's a political game for her."

"What is?"

"Life."

Which seemed suddenly not funny at all but just kind of sad. For her. For Bennet. Which was foolish. She'd grown up in a drug cartel. What could be sad about Bennet's picture-perfect political family?

"Why'd you give her a fake name when you introduced me?"

"Because her private investigators will be on you in five seconds. If you've ever stripped, inhaled, handed out fliers for minimum-wage increases, I will know it within the hour. But a fake name will slow her down."

"She checks out all your girlfriends?"

"All the ones I let her know about. Which is why I don't usually let her know. Which I imagine is why she's here at five in the morning and overly suspicious. But you don't have to worry."

"Because you didn't give her my real name?"

"Because I think you can eat my mother for lunch."

Alyssa glanced at the way the woman had gone.

She didn't think so. She might be a rough-and-tumble bounty hunter, but Mrs. Stevens had a cold fury underneath that spoke to being a lot tougher than she looked.

Still, Alyssa didn't mind Bennet thinking she could take his mother on.

"Let's head over to your office."

Alyssa nodded and followed along, but Bennet's mother haunted her for the rest of the day.

Chapter Five

"I can't find a damn thing," Bennet muttered. They'd spent over two hours searching Alyssa's office from top to bottom. Meticulously. They'd taken her desk apart, pulled at loose flooring, poked at soft drywall.

It was possible they'd overlooked something, but Bennet didn't have a clue as to what. Surely, surely the office had been bugged. How else would anyone have known to follow Alyssa last night?

He tried to push the frustration away, since it wouldn't get him any further in this case—and he'd already come further than he'd expected to in twenty-four hours—but something about knowing who the Jane Doe was, and who cared about her, made it seem all the more imperative to unravel this mystery.

Alyssa tossed some debris into a corner. "This is pointless. It could be anywhere. In anything."

"We've been through everywhere and everything. Maybe there was no bug."

"Then why would they have followed me last night?" She looked out her smudgy windows, frowning. Her profile reminded him of last night, when she'd stood in the middle of that parking lot and all but dared two thugs to harm her.

He shifted, trying to ignore the uncomfortable way his body reacted to that memory. "Maybe it's something else. Something seemingly unrelated. Had you ever seen those guys before?"

"No... Wait. Wait." She rushed over to her desk, pulling a crate off the floor.

"We already went through that."

She waved a hand. "Did you get the license plate off that car last night?"

"License plate. Make. Model. Picture on my phone."

"Pull it up."

He pulled out his phone and pulled up the information and placed it on the most level side of the desk. She pulled a little notebook from a seemingly endless supply of them and began rifling through it.

She found a page, read it, then glanced at his phone screen and swore. She shoved the notebook toward him, poking her finger at a few lines of chicken scratch. "I have seen those guys—well, their car. It was following me when I was on my last skip in Amarillo. Kept getting in my way. I thought it was friends of the skip trying to stop me, but..." She shook her head, forehead furrowed in confusion. "It is the same car. Same plate."

"So, your brothers have sent someone after you before, which means your office might not be bugged."

"But why? Why now?" She shoved her fingers into her hair, pulling some of the strands out of the band they were in. "Two years. I..." She trailed off, shaking her head, grappling with something bigger than this case.

She hardened her jaw, tossing the notebook back into her crate of notebooks. She stalked around the desk, shoving his phone back at him, something like fury in her gaze. A fury that definitely did not come from this alone.

"Okay, what's next?"

Bennet stilled. Next? Hell if he knew. He'd expected to find a bug and then go from there. He hadn't expected this twist.

"You're the Ranger. You have a plan. Don't you?"

"Why don't we take a deep breath and—"

"You *don't* have a plan."

"Alyssa—"

"You're probably not even really a Texas Ranger. Your mommy and daddy gave you a badge and everyone plays along. Pretends you aren't some idiotic—"

"Have a seat," he barked, gratified when she jumped a little.

"You don't order me around," she replied, lifting that chin, leveling him with that furious glare. It was only the fact there was some panicky undercurrent to it that he didn't bark out another order.

But he did advance, no matter how defiantly she kept his gaze. He stared her right down, getting up in her personal space until they were practically touching. "I said, have a seat," he growled.

Her screw-you expression didn't change, but she did blink and, after a few tense seconds, where he was thinking far too much about the shape of her mouth and not nearly enough about the threat he was trying to enact, she glanced behind her and pulled one of the folding chairs toward her.

She sat carefully, scowling at him all the way.

"I understand this is emotionally taxing for you, Alyssa." She scoffed, but he kept talking. "You will not lash out at me if you'd like me to allow you to—"

"Allow me, my a—"

She tried to stand up, but he took her by the shoulders and firmly pressed her back into the seat. "You're an asset, but don't forget you are working with me because I consider you one. Should you stop being one, I will no longer require your assistance."

"Perhaps," she said, speaking in the same way she had this morning when his mother had been around, mimicking a smooth, soft drawl, "I no longer require your assistance, Ranger Stevens." She shoved his hands off her shoulders with a flourish.

Which irritated him about as much as her words and her fake drawl and everything else about today that wasn't adding up.

So, he took her by the face, which was a mistake, his big palms against her soft cheeks. He felt her little inhale of breath, could see all too easily the way her pupils dilated as he bent over her.

He could feel the way her cheeks heated, the little puffs of breath coming out of her mouth, and there was an insane, blinding moment where he forgot what he was doing, why he was here. All he could think was that if he pressed his mouth to hers he'd know if she tasted as sharp as she always sounded.

He released her face and stepped back, shoving his hands into his pockets. "Getting pissed off at each other solves nothing. We need to arrange a meeting with your brothers somehow. Ferret out what they know." He paced, trying to focus on the information he had rather than the way the strands of her hair had felt trailing against the back of his hand. "Did your skip have something to do with them?"

"No," Alyssa said quietly. "At least, I don't think so."

"But he could have?"

She frowned in concentration. "I think I would have found a connection somewhere, something that rang familiar, but…"

"But what?" he demanded, no patience for her inward thinking that she wasn't sharing.

"I didn't know much about cartel business. I was kept very separated and very isolated from their world. My brothers always acted like I was in imminent danger. They told me if I ever went somewhere alone, there'd be a target on my chest. They were protecting me, they always said."

She seemed to doubt it now, in retrospect, and he couldn't help but wonder if they'd been so protective, so diligent in keeping her separate, then how had she been kidnapped? He hesitated to point that out, then berated himself for it.

He had an investigation to figure out. He could not be ignoring pertinent questions to spare her feelings. "How were you kidnapped?" he asked, gently. Softly. Certainly not in a tone befitting a Texas Ranger.

She hugged herself in that way she seemed to do only when she was really rattled, gaze sliding away from his. "I don't know," she whispered.

Something about that whisper, the vulnerable note, made the desperation wind inside him like a sharp, heavy rock, and he knew then and there he'd find out. He'd find out just how she'd come to be kidnapped, regardless of his case.

And if that was stupid and foolish, well, so be it.

ALYSSA DIDN'T WANT to talk about the kidnapping. She didn't want Bennet to talk to her in that gentle way that had to be a lie. Gentleness spoke to care, and all she was to him was a means to an end.

"What do you mean, you don't know?" he asked, and all of that fury and those hard edges from before when she'd insulted him and he'd ordered her to sit down were gone, softened into this…*concern*.

Which was too tempting, too alluring. She wanted to tell him everything, when she'd never told or wanted to tell anyone anything. Even Gabby knew only bits and pieces, because Alyssa didn't like to bring that pinched, pained look to her friend's face.

Gabby had been a prisoner for eight years. Nearly all of her twenties. It wasn't right. It wasn't fair.

But life never had been, Alyssa supposed. Which meant she had to tell Bennet the facts. She wouldn't let emotion get wrapped up in it. She'd just tell him what had happened, and if this had something to do with that…

She closed her eyes, trying to breathe, trying to work this all out in a way that made her want to act instead of cry.

"Take your time," Bennet said softly, giving her arm a quick squeeze, nothing like the way he'd grabbed her face and had those blue eyes boring into her, dropping to look at her mouth as though…

She snapped at him to keep her thoughts from traveling too far in that way-wrong direction. "Don't tell me what to do."

His mouth firmed, some of that softness going away, thank God.

"All I know about the kidnapping is one minute I was asleep in my bed, the next moment I woke up in the back of a van with a hood on my head. I was taken inside some giant warehouse, and there wasn't one person I recognized. A guy examined me, The Stallion, and I got taken to one of his little lairs."

"You would've had to have been drugged," Bennet said, focusing on the details of the kidnapping rather than the emotional scars as if he could read her mind and what she wanted.

"It's the only explanation," Alyssa replied. "I

just don't know…how. My brothers kept me locked away. *They* brought me my food. *They* protected me all those years. Before my mother disappeared. Before…" Well, she didn't feel right about letting Bennet in on their biggest family secret—that Dad wasn't in his right mind, or even in his right body. He was a shell in a locked-up room, just like she'd been.

"There's no way *they* could have arranged it?" Bennet asked, with something like regret on his face.

Or maybe that was projection, since she regretted this conversation, regretted and hated the doubts plaguing her. "Why would they protect me for twenty years, keep me safe and from harm, then with no warning hand me over to some crazy guy?" *Who only ever kept me as locked up as my brothers did.*

"I don't know," Bennet said carefully. "But if they protected you so well for twenty years, I don't understand why all the sudden you were kidnapped."

She swallowed at the lump in her throat and did everything she could to appear unaffected. "Well, neither do I."

"Come to think of it, the other night, they followed you. Not me. Alyssa, maybe this doesn't have anything to do with me and what I talked to you about, and everything to do with you."

She forced herself to breathe even though panic threatened to freeze her lungs. Why would it have to do with her? Why had they left her alone for *two* years? Why would they come *now*?

"I could be wrong," Bennet said, and he studied her with those soft eyes that made her want to punch him.

That's not really what you want to do with him.

She shook her head trying to focus, trying to *think*. "We need a next step," she said more to herself than him. "We need to get this over with so that I can enjoy Christmas with my…" She almost said "family." She'd let Gabby and Natalie become her family because her brothers hadn't come for her.

They'd left her. Abandoned her. And now they were back, lurking around the corners of her life.

Bennet reached out to touch her again, but before he could say anything, her door violently screeched open.

Two men in ski masks stepped inside, one with a very large gun, and when Bennet reached for his gun, they fired off a warning shot all too close to Bennet for Alyssa's comfort.

"On the ground," one of the men growled. Bennet didn't move, his face impassive, his hand on the butt of his weapon, though he didn't move another inch.

Alyssa knew she should move off her chair, should follow instructions, but Bennet's stoicism kept her calm, as did the way the man without the gun tapped long fingers against his thigh.

"I said get on the ground," the gunman said in that fake raspy voice.

Alyssa slowly stood, staring at the shape of the man's mouth, the breadth of his shoulders. The way he held that gun.

"Jose," Alyssa said, making sure it was clear she *knew* it was him, not just suspected. She glanced at the man without the gun, the brother closest in age to her. "Oscar. It's been a while."

Both men froze. Jose glanced at Oscar, still training the gun on Bennet. "How did she know it was us?" Jose demanded in a sad attempt at a whisper.

"I told CJ she wasn't stupid," Oscar muttered in disgust.

Alyssa swallowed at the odd lump in her throat, blinked at the stinging in her eyes. Four years. Four years ago her entire life had been torn from her, and now here was half of her entire life, the brothers who'd kept the closest tabs on her, in ski masks and with a gun.

Men she'd trusted her entire childhood to keep her safe. At least she'd always thought that's what they'd been doing. Had she been so wrong? So naive and stupid?

Two years she'd been imprisoned with that madman, The Stallion, and had slowly gone crazy realizing she'd *always* been imprisoned, for her entire life, but she'd waited. Waited to be rescued. To be found by the men she'd loved and trusted.

But she hadn't been rescued by them. She'd been rescued by the FBI. And for two years her brothers hadn't done a damn thing to contact her. They'd left her for dead.

Now, *now* they'd crashed back into her life and

were just *standing* there discussing whether CJ was right about her intelligence level.

Furious, and more than a little emotional, Alyssa stomped over to them and their sad little whispered argument. Jose's eyes widened, but he kept the gun trained on Bennet, who was standing calmly and placidly near where she'd been sitting.

She ignored Jose for the time being, and instead stood toe-to-toe with Oscar, her closest brother, her sweet and kind and caring closest brother, and slapped him across the face as hard as she could.

"What did you do that for?" Oscar howled, cradling his smacked cheek.

She tried to yell all the reasons why she'd hit him, but what she really wanted to do was cry, so she couldn't manage a yell, or anything more than a squeak.

She moved to slap Jose, too, for good measure, for mixing her up and making her want to cry, but before she could do anything, three more men stormed into the office.

Two with masks and guns just like Jose's went straight for Bennet. They jerked his arms behind his back and had him pressed to a wall, face-first, in seconds flat.

The other man stared straight at her, maskless, dark eyes cold and furious.

"I knew I couldn't trust you two," he muttered, glancing disgustedly at Jose and Oscar. "It's broad daylight. What the hell are you taking your time for? Eric, Benji, get the Ranger in the van. *Now.*"

"What about Alyssa?" Oscar asked, still cradling his cheek.

CJ, her eldest bother, the leader of the cartel, looked her over as if she was some kind of cargo. "Alyssa comes with me."

If she had any sense in her head, she'd let CJ take her. Her oldest brother had always been cold, remote and mostly ruthless, and it didn't make sense to cross him when she and Bennet had been planning on being taken anyway.

But slapping Oscar had only unleashed more fury rather than soothed any of it. She wanted to hit all of them. She wanted to beat them until they bled. She wanted answers, and hell if she was going to be calm or patient in the getting of them.

"Let him go," Alyssa said calmly and evenly, coolly even, matching CJ's cold stare with one of her own.

CJ leaned down, so close their noses almost touched. "Are you warming that Texas Ranger's bed, Alyssa? I didn't think we raised you to be a whore."

Those words, that tone, lit a fire to something inside her that had been simmering for all of these four years. She'd never acknowledged it, this blistering hurt and rage.

They'd abandoned her, to be kidnapped, to be let go. They'd given up any claim to her in four years of silence.

Now they had Bennet pressed to a wall with a gun to his head, and she wasn't stupid enough to think her brothers were *that* much stronger and smarter than him. No, Bennet was standing there *letting* them press him up against the wall.

For her.

No. No, for the *case*.

But it didn't matter, because she wasn't giving her brothers this kind of power. They'd run her life for years, but those years were over.

In a move she'd practiced for as long as she'd known how to walk, she pulled the gun out of her coat so swiftly, she had it shoved to CJ's gut before he'd even blinked an eye.

His mouth hardened, but he made no other reaction. "Am I supposed to believe you'd shoot me, my sweet Lyssie girl?"

She could almost believe he cared when he used that voice, that old nickname, but four years of separation had given her too many questions, too many doubts. "If you don't think I have the guts to shoot you right here, right now, then you don't know the woman you raised."

"You'd shoot your own brother? Whatever happened to loyalty?"

"Loyalty? You dare speak the word *loyalty* to me?" Alyssa shoved the gun against him harder, and he winced. "Family was supposed to be the only thing that mattered to you. Family was the rallying cry in *protecting* me. But I wasn't protected. I got kidnapped. I've been free from that for two years, and where have you been?"

"It's complicated," CJ growled.

"It's not. You weren't there, and now I don't need you." She looked down at the gun in her hand, surprised to find herself steady. When she looked back up at CJ, she smiled. "But I may spare your life."

CJ scoffed. "Jose, give me that gun."

"I'll shoot him if you move, Jose. And what would the world do without CJ Jimenez in it to pull its strings?"

"What do you want?" CJ asked, feigning boredom, but Alyssa could see a faint line of concern on his forehead.

She fiddled with the safety of her gun, just to show him she wasn't messing around. "Our mother was murdered, and I want to know why."

CJ's mouth curved and his gaze moved to Bennet, who somehow looked calm and model-like pressed to her grimy office wall. "I think your Ranger has a few more answers about these things than he lets on."

Alyssa didn't jerk, didn't react, though inwardly her stomach tightened into a painful cramp. Had Bennet been lying to her? Someone was. It could be him. But CJ was her impending doom right now, and she had to take care of him first.

"Drop the guns, let the Ranger go, or I shoot CJ. I'll count to ten."

She watched as her brothers all stood wide-eyed

and frozen as she counted down. Finally, CJ inclined his head. "Let the Ranger go," he grumbled.

"And drop the guns. Now."

The two brothers holding Bennet let go, slowly putting their guns on the ground along with Jose. Bennet didn't scurry away, didn't scowl, didn't outwardly react in any way. He simply picked the guns up and used the straps to sling them onto his shoulder.

"I want you all lined up in front of the door," Alyssa said, pushing CJ back toward the door with the gun.

They scrambled to do her bidding, and Alyssa couldn't ignore the thrill it gave her. She was in charge. *She* had outwitted them. *She* was going to get what *she* wanted for once. For damn once.

And there they were. All five of them. The men she'd loved and trusted for her entire life.

She'd spent the past two years fearing they didn't love her. Being so afraid she didn't matter or that they thought she was tainted in some way. But none of that fear or sadness was inside her right now. All she felt was rage. Rage that they'd abandoned her. After giving her very few skills with which to survive—only violence and suspicion.

Bennet came to stand behind her, and she expected him to tell her what to do. She didn't know what, but she expected *something*. He hadn't uttered a word this entire altercation.

He still didn't. He just stood there. Behind her. A

calming, supportive force. Because it was her turn. *Her* turn to be in charge of her life.

"I want all the information you have on my kidnapping and our mother's murder. And if I think you're lying, I'll pick you off one by one."

"And I'll help," Bennet added cheerfully, holding one of the guns in his hands, sights set on CJ.

Chapter Six

For a few moments Bennet could only stand behind Alyssa and stare. He hadn't known she had a gun on her. How could he have missed that, and what kind of Ranger did it make him that he had?

But that moderate shame was no match for the other feeling that assailed him. Awe. She'd fended off an attack from all five of her brothers. Who did that? They were the leaders of a *cartel*, three of them had guns, and yet she'd gotten them to drop their weapons, all without his having to lift a finger.

He'd been content to let her brothers think they had the upper hand, eager for them to pull him into their world so he could find his answers.

But Alyssa had a gun on them and point-blank asked for those answers, and so he'd stood behind her and backed her up. It was the only thing to do.

"Why don't you ask your Ranger, Lyss?" the clear leader of the group said, dark eyes zeroed in on him.

Alyssa didn't flick so much as a glance back at him, but he saw the way her shoulders tensed, the way CJ insinuating Bennet knew something he wasn't telling her bothered her.

"If I knew anything about either, I wouldn't be here," Bennet replied coolly.

CJ cocked his head, and even if Bennet didn't know about her brothers and their documented work in cartel dealings, he'd know this man was dangerous. Powerful.

But this man had cowered to Alyssa, and that was something to use.

"When are you going to run for office like Mommy and Daddy, Ranger boy?" CJ asked.

Something prickled at the back of Bennet's neck, that telltale gut feeling something was seriously wrong, but he didn't have enough to bluff his way through this one. So, he had to go with the truth. "I'm not a politician."

"Hmm." CJ considered Bennet as if two guns weren't pointed at him. "And I suppose the name Sal Cochrane means nothing to you."

Bennet racked his brain, every memory, every case, every person he'd ever met, but he came up blank.

"Salvador Dominguez, then?"

Bennet was very careful to keep the recognition off his face. The Dominguez cartel was newer and less powerful than the Jimenez one, but it had been gaining in power of late. But who the hell was Sal Cochrane?

CJ kept studying him, but Bennet didn't know

what the man was looking for. What the man thought Bennet knew.

"Politics is dirty business, Ranger Stevens," CJ said, putting extra emphasis on his last name, and there was that scalp prickle again. Foreboding.

"I suppose it is, but like I said, I'm not a politician. That's my parents."

"I guess we'll see," CJ murmured.

"Who the hell are you here for, CJ?" Alyssa demanded. "Me or him?"

CJ's mouth curved in what Bennet assumed was supposed to be a smile. "If I wanted either of you, I'd have you."

Which sent a cold chill down Bennet's spine, because he was beginning to realize this was all a little too easy. For five men involved in a drug cartel with an insane amount of weaponry, one woman—sister or not, remarkable or not—they hadn't actually been bested.

This was all an act. Bennet kept his gun aimed at CJ, but he started looking around. There was a back entrance, but he'd not just locked it when they'd entered through it, he'd barred the door. They at least couldn't be ambushed without warning that way.

Alyssa shoved the gun in CJ's gut again, with enough force that CJ coughed out a breath. "Why was I kidnapped?" she demanded. "You're not leaving here without telling me. How the hell did someone drug me and get me out of the house?"

CJ's mouth firmed, and the one who'd come inside without a gun stared at his feet. Whatever the reason, these men all knew it, which meant they were probably part of it.

Which, unfortunately, Bennet knew would hurt Alyssa immeasurably. She'd seen them as her protectors all this time, and not coming after her had been a betrayal—even if Bennet thought she was better off without them—but this?

"You never came for me," Alyssa replied, and on the surface her voice was calm, collected, but there was something vibrating underneath, something Bennet figured she was trying to hide. Emotion. Hurt. "And now you're here spouting threats at *him*. What is this?"

"Still dying to be the center of attention after all these years, Lyssie?"

Bennet opened his mouth to say something, anything to put the man in his place, but that's when he saw a flicker of light outside the grimy windows, and when the glass exploded seconds later, he couldn't be sure what was coming through, but he knew it wasn't good.

And far too close to Alyssa. He lunged for her, knocking her onto the ground and underneath him. He couldn't make out whatever words of protest she was making, because something exploded.

He could feel heat, bits of debris painfully pelting his back and Alyssa breathing underneath him.

She was swearing, pushing at him, but breathing. In and out. Bennet was almost afraid to see what had caused the explosion, afraid to see what casualties there might be, but he could still feel the heat on his back, which meant the place was on fire.

He pushed off her and onto his feet, offering his hand to help her up, but she scrambled past him unaided.

"Where'd they go?" She stared at the door and the flames licking around it. None of her brothers or her brothers' bodies were anywhere to be seen. There was only a line of flame slowly spreading down the length of the front wall.

She whirled on him. "Where'd they go?"

"Alyssa…"

"You let them get away. You…" She slapped her palms to his chest and pushed. Hard, and while in normal circumstances it wouldn't have hurt him in the least, a searing pain shot through his shoulder and back at his body's movement.

He hissed out a breath, and some of her desperate fury was replaced by confusion, and maybe concern. She tried to move past him, but he moved with her, keeping his back hidden.

"We need to get out of here," he said, sucking in a smoky breath before reaching his arm out to take hers. To usher her out the back way. The fire wasn't huge, but they needed to get out before the smoke got worse, and they really needed to leave before anyone saw them.

He nudged her in front of him, pushing her down

the hall no matter how often she scowled over her shoulder at him. He pulled the heavy rack he'd pushed in front of the back door earlier away, no matter how his back screamed, then pushed her out the door and into the alley where they'd parked his car.

He wasn't sure how he was going to drive like this, but they had to get out of here before they were seen. If he had to explain this to the Rangers, other law enforcement would be brought in, and he wasn't ready for that yet. Not when he knew so little.

Not when CJ Jimenez had dropped hints about his parents.

No, he had to figure out what this whole thing was about before anyone else got involved. If his parents were connected to something... He could hardly stomach the thought, but he wouldn't protect them. He couldn't. Not at the cost of everything he'd sworn himself to.

But he had to be sure first.

"Oh my God. You're bleeding," Alyssa gasped when he passed her to head for the driver's side.

Bennet paused and glanced down his back as best he could. "It's just some glass," he muttered.

"We have to get you to a hospital."

"No," he said, leveling her with his most serious glare. "We have to get the hell out of here."

"Bennet, there are *shards* of glass sticking out of your back. How do you suggest we get the hell out of here?"

He looked down at the keys in his hand and then shrugged, wincing in pain. He tossed her his keys, trying not to show how the move hurt him. "You're driving."

Alyssa drove Bennet's fancy car through the streets of Austin, back to his parents' guesthouse, glancing occasionally in the rearview mirror to the back seat, where Bennet was pretzeled into a position where his back wouldn't hit anything.

It looked awful, and Alyssa was half-tempted to drive him to the hospital against his will.

But none of this made sense. Not her brothers' appearance, not their disappearance and not Bennet's refusal to stick around and deal with it as an official law enforcement agent. He'd called 911 and given the pertinent information, but not his name.

Luckily she didn't really care if her office burned to the ground. She still had her gun and her motorcycle, which were the most important possessions she owned. The paperwork she kept in the office was helpful, but not necessary. The few important documents she had, she kept in a safe-deposit box at the bank. Losing the office meant nothing.

Losing out on answers meant everything.

She glanced at Bennet again as she drove the long, winding drive to his parents' guesthouse after he'd ground out the code to the gate and she'd punched it in.

She supposed that man meant a little bit. He'd

certainly jumped between her and harm. She could be the one with shards of glass sticking out of her if he hadn't acted so quickly.

As much as she might want to blame Bennet for letting her brothers get away, she wasn't stupid. Everything that had happened—from her knowing Jose and Oscar on sight even with masks, to the fire-bomb that allowed the Jimenez brothers to escape—had all been part of a plan.

CJ hadn't given her any information he hadn't wanted to, and while he'd given her nothing, he'd planted all sorts of new doubts about Bennet in her head.

She parked the car at the garage door and pulled the keys from the ignition. "Let me guess, you have a magic doctor on staff who's going to stitch all that up?"

"No, I'm afraid that's going to have to fall to you. Hope you're not squeamish." On a grunt, he shoved the door open. Wincing and breathing a little too heavily, he maneuvered himself out of the car without any help.

Alyssa scrambled to do just that—help. No matter what insinuations CJ had made, this man had stepped between her and an explosion. His first instinct had been to protect her, which was not an instinct apparently any of her brothers shared. And even before all that, Bennet had given her something no man in her entire life had ever given her: power.

He'd let her hold a gun on her brothers and question them without stepping in, without riding roughshod. He'd given her space, and he'd protected her.

Maybe he knew more than he'd let on, but she wasn't about to let CJ manipulate her into doing what *he* wanted. No, she was going to make up her own mind. Slowly. Carefully. Once she had all the evidence laid out before her.

She followed Bennet inside, through the vast white rooms and plush hallways and into a bathroom that was about the size of her entire above-the-garage apartment.

He bent over, hissing out a breath as he pulled a white box out from under the sink. He dropped it on the beautiful countertop. "First aid kit. I doubt there will be anything to pull the glass out with, though."

Alyssa unzipped her jacket and turned slightly away from Bennet. Once her front was shielded from his view, she pulled her Swiss Army knife out of her bra before turning around and holding it up. "I've got tweezers."

His mouth curved, and his little exhale of breath was something close to a laugh. "Of course you do." He reached behind him and tugged at his collar, but winced and dropped it. "Help me get this off," he ground out, turning his back to her again.

The shirt was ruined—torn, bloody—and if she focused on that she would maybe not focus on the fact he'd just asked her to help him take his shirt off.

"I, uh, should maybe get some of the glass out

first." Which was the truth, not some excuse to keep from having to touch his naked back.

"Go for it."

"Right." She blew out a breath and ignored how her hand shook as she pulled the tweezer tool out of her Swiss Army knife.

She had to splay her hand across the least torn-up shoulder blade to try to find her balance and leverage. Some of the tenseness in his shoulder relaxed at her touch, and she didn't know what to make of that. That or the too-hard beating of her heart.

She took a deep breath and focused on the largest piece of glass sticking out of Bennet's back. She bit her lip and used the tweezers to pull it out. Bennet didn't move, didn't make a sound. She placed the stomach-curdling piece of bloody glass on the sink, wincing a little at the thought of the blood staining the countertop.

"Well, I think it might look worse than it actually is," Alyssa offered hopefully, shuffling awkwardly closer to get the next piece of glass.

"Great," Bennet muttered.

"This would be easier with you lying on a bed."

He glanced at her over his shoulder, something about the wide-eyed look and slight curve of his mouth causing her face to heat.

"J-just for…leverage."

His mouth curved even more. "Leverage," he repeated, far too amused.

She scowled at him. "You want this glass out of you or not?"

"The bed it is. You want to take my shirt off first?"

She pretended to study his back if only so she didn't have to meet his gaze. "All right," she said, refusing to let any of her uncertainty come out in her voice.

She flexed her fingers, willing away the slight tremor in them before touching the hem of his T-shirt. She could do this. Take some glass out of his back, take off a shirt. It was all just…business.

Sort of.

She swallowed and pulled the shirt away from Bennet's back, then lifted the fabric. "You're, uh, going to have to bend over or pull it or something."

He reached back with only a minimal sucked-in breath and pulled the shirt off, leaving his back completely bare. And broad. And strong. And bloody.

"Oh." His injuries weren't anywhere near serious, but it looked so ugly. Glass and blood and scratches. She touched her finger to an unmarred spot, feeling oddly protective, hurt by this silly little attack on him.

"Not looking so great now?"

She pulled her hand away, something like guilt washing over her. "You'll live."

He made a considering noise then gestured toward a second door. "To the bed, then?" And somehow this man with bits of glass shards in his back was grinning at her. Charmingly.

She'd faced down her brothers, a madman of a kidnapper and all his goons, a parcel of FBI agents in an attempt to garner some power, admittedly foolish in retrospect. She'd faced all those people down without a qualm, but it was always the quiet moments she didn't know what to do with.

Gabby and Natalie's kindness. A charming smile from an all-too-handsome Texas Ranger. It made her feel young and stupid.

She grabbed the first aid kit and lifted her chin at him. "I'll follow you."

He walked out the door and into a huge bedroom, all white and black just like every other room in his bizarre place. Where was the color? The charm? The—

Bennet got on the bed, lying stomach down on the pristine white blankets. He crossed his hands under his head and rested his temple on the back of one hand, studying her.

She looked away and placed the kit on the nightstand and focused on getting out and opening bandages and not staring at a Texas Ranger all sprawled out half-naked on his bed after saving her from... well, minor injury.

"I do have an investigation to start if we could hurry this damn thing up."

"Right." Except he was lying there, and she wasn't sure why she thought this would give her more leverage. Oh, she could reach all places on his back easier, but she'd have to lean over him. Brush against him. Hell, it'd be easiest if she could just straddle his legs and go at it that way.

She was *not* going to go at it that way. But she did have to do it. So, enough of being a silly little girl. Maybe she was a sheltered virgin in the oddest sense of the word, but she had a job to do. Bennet had helped her out, and now it was her turn to help him.

So, she focused on the glass shards and pulling out all she could see. She focused on using the antibiotic ointment on the cuts and bandaging them up. And if she noticed that his skin was soft, or that his muscles rippled appealingly any time he moved, well… So what? Adult women did that sort of thing, didn't they? Noticed attractive men.

"There might still be debris in there," Alyssa said, bandaging up the last of the cuts. "I only got out what I could see."

"It'll be good enough," he replied, pushing himself into a sitting position on the bed.

"You should go to the hospital. Some of those bigger cuts might need stitches."

He shook his head.

"Why aren't you reporting this?" There was a reason, and she was a little afraid she knew what it was.

His jaw firmed, but he didn't look away. That blue gaze pinned her in place. "First off, they'd put me on medical leave for a day or two and give someone else the case. Second of all…"

"Your parents?"

"That was your brother's insinuation."

"And you believe him?"

Bennet looked away for a moment. "I don't know. It could be a trick. It could be true. It could be a lot of things, but I want to be the one to figure it out."

"I should go."

He looked back at her, brow furrowing. "Go where?"

"Home. No one was bugging my place, and my brothers didn't hurt me or take me, which means they aren't going to. There's no reason for me to stay here."

He scooted to the edge of the bed and took her hands with his before she could think to step away. "Alyssa, that doesn't mean you're not in danger," he said seriously.

"I've been in danger before. I can handle myself."

He studied her, and she couldn't read his expression or guess what he was looking for, but when she tried to tug her hands away, he only held on tighter.

"I know your brothers insinuated that I know something about your mother, about anything, but I don't. You have to believe that."

"I do." Maybe she shouldn't, but why would he have come to her with her mother's picture as a Jane Doe if he knew anything?

"If either of my parents is involved in some kind

of crime, I will not hesitate to turn them in, Alyssa. I took an oath. For what it's worth, my parents took an oath, and if they are not representing their constituents in a lawful fashion, then it's out of my hands."

She blinked at the vehemence in his tone. "O-okay."

"So you don't need to worry."

"What do you think I'm worried about?"

"You're trying to leave. You must be worried about something."

"I'm… You don't need me, Bennet. You got your Jane Doe name, and there's no point trying to get drawn into my brothers' world now. They know too much." She was useless to him. *Just like you're useless to everyone else.*

Again she tugged her hands, but Bennet held her in his grasp.

"Until we know how this all connects, until we can be certain you're safe, you're under my protection."

Tears pricked her eyes unexpectedly. Protection. She was so tired of being under someone else's protection. And yet, today Bennet had let her fight her own battle within that protection. He hadn't abandoned her or allowed her to be hurt like everyone else had.

"And you're right, we can't go into your brothers' world now, but we have a much bigger challenge ahead of us," he said gravely.

We. *We.* As if they were a team, working together,

protecting each other. "We do?" she managed to ask past the lump in her throat.

"I have to bring you into mine."

Chapter Seven

Bennet didn't bother to find a new shirt, and he didn't bother to try to figure out what Alyssa's silence meant. They had work to do.

"Did you recognize either of the names your brother mentioned?"

Alyssa blew out a breath. "Sal Cochrane not so much."

"And Salvador Dominguez?"

Her expression shuttered, and he supposed it was answer enough, though it didn't sit well with him that she knew.

"I've been a bounty hunter—"

"Illegal bounty hunter," he interrupted, because he liked the way she scowled at him when he did. "You don't only know Dominguez from the past two years. Don't insult me with a lie at this point."

She had the decency to look a little shamed. "I don't know Salvador Dominguez, but I have heard of him."

"From your brothers?"

She shook her head almost imperceptibly.

"Then from who?" he demanded, as irritated with her hesitation as he was with the burning sensation in his back.

"My father, but…" Alyssa rubbed her hands together, clearly working out something in her head without letting him in on pertinent information.

"But what?"

"He wasn't… He isn't… When he told me about Dominguez, none of it made any sense. And when I told CJ, he…"

"He what?"

Her gaze flew to his. "Oh my God. He made me think Dad was crazy. He convinced me Dad had lost his mind but… But Dad said Salvador Dominguez had our mother. That she hadn't left, that someone had double-crossed him and *I* would be next and… Bennet, they convinced me Dad was crazy, but maybe he wasn't."

"Why tell us? And what does it have to do with Sal Cochrane?"

She shook her head, eyebrows drawn together, hands clasped. "I don't know. I don't know." She paced, fury taking over her features. "I hate that we have to find out when that's just what he wants us to do."

"Maybe it's some kind of warning. Some kind of way to help you, and if we find out—"

She laughed. Bitterly. "I might be able to convince myself of that if it had been any of my other brothers, but CJ has been in charge too long to have any decency left in him. Whatever reason he has for showing up, for letting me go, for dropping those little breadcrumbs, it is for the cartel's well-being and that alone."

She wrapped her arms around herself, and he curled his hands into fists so he didn't reach out. They could probably stand a little less touching, a little less close quarters, and a lot less his being an idiot and trying to make her blush.

How this unbelievably strong fighter of a woman could *blush* at the remotest sexual thing was beyond him, and he liked it far too much.

But *sexual* was not something he could afford to be thinking about. No matter how gently she'd tended his wounds, or how brave she was, or how much he wanted to protect her.

"Does The Stallion have anything to do with the cartels?" she asked, still hugging her arms around herself.

"The Stallion has been in prison for two years," he reminded her as gently as he could.

"Before that, I mean. It all has to connect, don't you think? Not just now, either. This is sixteen years in the making, if it connects to my mother."

Bennet sighed. He didn't know. It seemed there were a million connections and he didn't have a clue about any of them. It was more than possible a rival cartel could have killed Alyssa's mother, but that didn't explain why she'd been left a Jane Doe.

There were too many unanswered questions, and what clues he had came from criminals with their own agendas. If he thought he'd been frustrated at the prospect of a Jane Doe, it had nothing on *this* frustration.

But this was what he wanted. A challenge. To do something good for once. All on his own.

"Bennet," a voice boomed from the entryway.

Bennet swore. The last thing he wanted to do right now was go toe-to-toe with his father.

"I assume that's not the staff," Alyssa offered drily.

"It's my father."

"Do your parents know how to knock?"

"Not if it doesn't suit them." Bennet glanced at the door. It was no use to hide Alyssa when Mother would have already told Father about her, but he didn't want to waste time trading fake niceties or old-hat arguments with his father.

He took a step toward Alyssa. There was one possible way to get his father out of here quickly. And he was already shirtless.

"I need you to go along with something, all right?"

"With what? Being Alyssa Clark? I did this morning. I don't see why…"

She trailed off when he slid his arms around her, her eyes widening as she looked up at him.

"W-what are you doing?"

"We need time, and if my father comes in here he won't be sweeping out anytime soon. Not like my mother. He'll want to stay and chat and charm and who knows what all. We don't have time for that, so we're going to pretend we are otherwise engaged."

"Bennet?" the voice boomed again, closer.

"Otherwise. Engaged," Alyssa repeated breathlessly, and though she leaned away from him she didn't jerk away or try to escape.

So, he pulled her close and lowered his mouth close to hers. "It's only pretend. Like…undercover work."

Her eyelashes fluttered and her breath came in short bursts, and he had no business wondering if the attraction he felt wasn't one-sided. If she might feel some of that in return. If she might…

"Bennet?" This time followed by a knock on the bedroom door as the knob turned.

Bennet pressed his mouth to Alyssa's, but all she did was stand there. Frozen and wide-eyed and not at all pretending. She didn't slap him either, but she didn't relax or even feign a kiss back.

"You have to kiss me back," he whispered across her mouth.

"B-but I don't know how."

Hell.

BENNET WAS KISSING HER. His mouth was on her mouth, and no matter that he held her sturdily against him, that he'd called it pretend, she didn't know what the hell to do with her mouth or her arms or with anything.

His father was stepping inside the room and—Bennet's fingers tangled in her hair, angling her whole head so that his mouth slid more easily across hers. Sweetly. Gently. It was warm and…nice. Nice enough to relax into, to soften. She very nearly sighed.

So, this was kissing. Well, she supposed having her body pressed up against the large, hard body of a man while his soft, firm mouth angled over hers had its appeal. It made her whole body feel warm and heavy, it made every place her body touched his seem to sparkle to life, and to taste another person—

A throat cleared, and Alyssa jerked. She didn't know how she'd lost so much track of where she was or what…

She could only blink up at Bennet, but his expression was blank, his jaw hard and his gaze not on her.

"Sorry to interrupt," an unfamiliar voice drawled, sounding very much not sorry.

Alyssa finally gathered enough sense to step away from Bennet and look at their intruder. Which made Alyssa blink all over again.

"*Are* you sorry to interrupt, Father?" Bennet asked, his voice cool and unaffected. "Because a gentleman would perhaps just step back out."

Mr. Stevens smiled widely and looked so much like his son Alyssa could only stare.

"Gary L. Stevens," he said in that charming drawl, holding out a hand to her. And Alyssa would have to give him credit. He might have worse timing than Bennet's mother, but he was certainly kinder.

"I would really prefer it if you weren't introducing yourself to women in my bedroom when we are in the middle of something."

"So traditional," Mr. Stevens said with a wink to Alyssa.

"What are you doing here? I am busy," Bennet said through gritted teeth.

"Your mother sent me on a fact-finding mission, and you know how she gets. I wasn't about to return empty-handed. You must be Alyssa. Clark, was it?"

Alyssa nodded mutely. Where Mrs. Stevens had put her back up with her cold disapproval, she didn't know what to do with Mr. Stevens's easy friendliness. Much like she didn't know what to do with Bennet's fake kisses that apparently affected him not at all.

"I know it's incredibly rude of me, Ms. Clark, but I need just a few moments in private with my son or I'll never get any peace at home."

Bennet opened his mouth, presumably to argue, but Alyssa didn't think that would do anyone any good. She adopted her smooth, fake drawl and smiled sweetly at Mr. Stevens. "Of course." She glanced at Bennet, reminded herself she was playing a part. And the part was that of possible floozy girlfriend.

She patted his bare chest and attempted to look pouty and alluring even though she had no idea how to look that. "You might want to put a shirt on, honey."

Especially if he was going to keep the injuries hidden from his father.

Alyssa walked out the door, pulling it almost closed behind her, but she left a crack. When no one finished closing it, she took a few steps down the hall, then stood exactly where she was, gratified when she could hear everything being said.

"Her last name isn't Clark," Mr. Stevens offered with no preamble.

"You think I don't know that?"

Mr. Stevens sighed heavily. "Your mother is having a conniption."

"Then everything's normal, I assume."

"She wants a name."

"She won't get it from me."

"If the girl has nothing to hide, let your mother run her little background checks. And if she does have something to hide, well, you know your mother won't go exposing her. It would only look poorly on us."

"Regardless of what's in her background, I don't want you two poking around in it or coming after her. She is none of your business. If Mother can't get that through her head after all this time, I don't know what to tell you."

"And yet you're here, under our roof."

Alyssa edged closer to the door, trying to see through the crack in the door. She could see a sliver of Bennet—who'd pulled on a sweatshirt at some point—but she couldn't see his father. She couldn't help but be curious about what Mr. Stevens's reaction might be to that cold fury in Bennet's expression. And, more, she couldn't understand Bennet's relationship with his parents.

She knew her family was warped beyond belief, and she knew that her brothers fought, sometimes furiously, over cartel business, but she'd assumed that was the life of criminals. Not the life of someone like Bennet and his parents.

"What do you know about Sal Cochrane?" Bennet asked with no finesse, no easing into it. Alyssa frowned. Couldn't he be smoother than all that?

"Is that a friendly question, son, or an official one?" Mr. Stevens returned easily.

"Is that a political evasion or you just being difficult?"

After another long sigh, Mr. Stevens answered. "He's one of your mother's silent donors, I believe. Never met the man myself, so that's about all I know. You're not going to bring your mother into trouble."

Which was not a question. Even Alyssa knew that from her eavesdropping spot in the hall.

"If she isn't already in any."

"Bennet, we've never stood in your way when it came to police work or joining the Rangers. We've never—"

"I'm not going after Mother," Bennet interrupted, clearly irritated by his father's line of conversation.

He stepped out of her slim view through the crack in the door. "Sal Cochrane is who I'm after, and it's only for information, so if you have any information, I'd appreciate it. Officially."

"I'll see what I can do." Mr. Stevens stepped into view. "In return for that young woman's last name."

Bennet made a scoffing noise, and Mr. Stevens turned his head, in a seemingly casual move. But as Alyssa didn't have time to move out of the way, she doubted there was anything casual about it.

He'd either known she was there or suspected it, and she wasn't stupid enough to believe Mr. Stevens hadn't caught her spying. Crap.

Still, better to give the illusion she didn't know she'd been caught. She hurried as silently as possible down the hall and to the bedroom she'd slept in last night. She desperately wanted to listen to the rest of that conversation, to see if Bennet would trade her name for the information he wanted, but as she stepped into the blindingly white room, she realized she had bigger fish to fry.

"What are you doing here? How did you get in?"

Oscar smiled sheepishly. "Hi, sis."

"You...you can't be here." It would be bad enough if Bennet saw him, but if Mr. Stevens saw him, too? Alyssa didn't have a clue as to what might happen, but she knew it wouldn't be good. At the very least her brother would be arrested, and while he might be deserving of that...

Oscar had snuck her checkers and Baby-Sitters

Club books. He'd given her sweets and taken her on walks when none of her other brothers would. He'd treated her like a girl, a sister, not just a possession. A statue to protect.

She couldn't let anything happen to Oscar. Not like this. She grabbed him by the arm and tried to pull him toward the door, but he jerked out of her grasp.

"I don't have time, but I had to warn you. Don't try to figure this out. Don't get involved. Stay low, get your Ranger to stay low, and you'll be fine. But if you let CJ drag you into this, you will get hurt."

"Drag me into what?"

"I'm risking my life here, Alyssa. That's all I can say."

"Os—"

But before she could even get the words out of her mouth, he was climbing out the window Alyssa hadn't realized was open. She might have followed him, she might have grabbed him again, but she could hear footsteps in the hall and she couldn't risk being discovered.

"Alyssa!" Oscar hissed from outside.

She pushed the curtains back and looked at her brother standing in the perfectly manicured yard of the Stevenses' guesthouse, a figure all in black, the faint scar across his cheek he'd never told her how he'd gotten.

"Don't tell your Ranger I was here. Please." And

then he was gone, running silently around the corner of the house.

"Well, I hope you know how to clean up," Bennet said, and Alyssa whirled away from the window. Probably the only thing saving her from being caught was the fact Bennet's attention was on a card in his hand.

"Clean up?" she echoed stupidly, her heart hammering a hundred times in overdrive.

He looked up at her, that charming smile so easily camouflaging his true emotions.

"We're going to a ball, Cinderella."

Chapter Eight

Bennet sat at the kitchen table, casually eating his dinner, while Alyssa continued to rant. And rant. And rant, rant, rant. It was almost amusing, really, considering he'd watched this woman fly down a highway on a motorcycle waving at very bad men, watched this woman hold a gun on her brothers, and yet those weren't the things that caused her to come unglued.

No, she was losing it at the prospect of going to one of his parents' idiotic Christmas balls or galas or whatever they were calling this one.

"I'm not going."

"Yes, you are."

"I don't work for you, Bennet."

"No, but you're working with me."

"Are you always this infuriatingly unruffled?"

He shrugged, grinning at her. "When it suits." He hadn't been unruffled this afternoon. Not with his father, and certainly not with Alyssa and the kiss.

The *fake* kiss. That had made him far more irri-

table with his father than he should have been. Too
direct. Too…everything.

"Maybe we shouldn't," Alyssa said, and when he
looked up at her, she had her back to him while she
pretended to make herself a sandwich. Pretended because she'd been doing so for the last twenty minutes
without finishing.

"Maybe we shouldn't what?"

He watched her shoulders lift and fall as though
she was inhaling deeply, steeling herself for something. She turned, and though she looked at him,
he got the distinct impression she was staring at his
nose instead of meeting his actual gaze.

"Maybe we shouldn't work together. Work…pe-
riod. If my mother's death was cartel business, what
does it matter?"

Bennet stood slowly. "It's an unsolved murder
case, that's what it matters." He narrowed his eyes
at her. Suddenly she was fidgety, and backing off,
and that was very much not the Alyssa Jimenez he'd
come to know in a short few days.

So maybe you don't know her at all.

"You said yourself that CJ *wants* us to find this
all out, and I'm worried about playing into that trap."
She hugged her arms around her even as she kept
looking at him defiantly. But something had rattled
her, and Bennet wasn't about to let her get away
with it.

"Why?"

"What do you mean *why*? Did it escape your notice my brother is a dangerous man?"

"Who didn't hurt you when he had the chance."

"That doesn't mean he won't ever hurt me or..."

"Or what?"

"Or you, idiot," she snapped. "He wants us to go looking for this information, but what will happen if we find it? Why can't he find it himself? It's stupid to go after it. It's like helping him."

Bennet took a few steps toward her, and no matter that what she said held some truth, this was all a sudden change from how she'd been earlier. A woman didn't change her mind like this without provocation. "Alyssa. What happened?"

"Noth—"

He curled his fingers around her shoulders and cut her off. "Do not lie to me again. What happened?"

She swallowed, but she didn't lose that defiant tilt to her chin. "It isn't safe to go after this, and I don't want to go to your dumb ball."

"Is that all this is, Princess? Don't want to wear a dress?"

"It isn't funny."

"Then what is it?"

"Dangerous! And not just to us, or to my family, but to your parents. CJ wants to bring them into this. All of us. Why are we falling for it?"

"And why are you suddenly skittish?" Something inside him went past irritation to worry, but that only served to irritate him. He had no business worrying about her state of mind. He had a case to solve.

She gave him a push, stalking past him, though she didn't leave the kitchen, just started pacing across it.

"Alyssa, we'll get nowhere if you lie to me."

Her breathing hitched, and a little sob escaped, and no matter how clearly she tried to fight back the tears, they slipped down her cheeks.

"I don't know who to trust. Who to believe," she said in a squeaky voice, tears tracking down her jaw.

Bennet knew he should keep his hands to himself, but he'd known a lot of things in his life that feeling had taken over, and this was no different. He stepped toward her and brushed the tears off her cheeks. "I know what that's like, and I know I can't make you believe or trust me, but I haven't let you down yet, have I?"

She shook her head.

"I grew up in a world of lies and deception, where it mattered more what people thought than what people did. 'Oh, Mr. So-and-So beats his wife, but the checks he writes for the campaign are quite large, so we'll look the other way.' I hated it, always, so I sought out the exact opposite of that world. Not truth, not honesty, but—"

"Justice," she finished for him in a whisper.

He blinked at her, but he shouldn't have been shocked she understood. She'd grown up in a cartel, and since her kidnapping release had built a bounty hunter business. It might not be legal, but it was a search for justice.

Just like him.

He should stop touching her face, and he would. In a minute or two. "Yeah, I guess you know something about that, don't you?"

"Oscar was here," she said in a whisper.

His hands dropped from her wet face. "What?"

"While you were talking to your father. He…he was in my room. He told me not to listen to CJ. That it was dangerous."

Bennet wanted to yell at her, demand to know why she'd kept it from him for *hours*. Demand everything, but he'd seen that look on her face in so many victims he'd come across in his work.

Fear, and—worse, so much worse—a kind of grim acceptance that pain and suffering were just around the corner.

So, he swallowed down his anger, flexed his fingers from the fists they wanted to curl into. He breathed evenly, doing his best to unclench his jaw. "And you believe him?"

"Oscar was always the nicest of all of them. The one with a heart, if you can believe it. There'd be no nefarious reason to warn me off. No self serving ones. He was trying to warn me so CJ didn't hurt me. Didn't hurt both of us. He told me not to tell you, Bennet. He's afraid, too. If CJ found out…" She closed her eyes as if she couldn't bear to think about it.

"I know they're your brothers, but I need you on my team, Alyssa. I need your eyes, and I need your brain and memories. I need you to be in this with me so we can find out what happened to your mother, and to you. Justice. For both of you. But you have to trust me, and if Oscar contacts you again, I have to know you'll tell me. I have to be able to trust you. It is necessary."

She used the back of her hand to wipe off her cheek.

"Is there anything else you're keeping from me?"

She looked up at the ceiling as if she was shuffling through all her memories of what she might have kept from him. She eventually shook her head. "No. You've been with me every moment except that one."

"And last night."

"I was sleeping last night," she said, her tear-stained cheeks turning an appealing shade of pink.

There was something seriously warped with him. He should still be angry. He should be nervous and worried and thinking about Sal Cochrane.

But all he could think about was that kiss. *Fake kiss. Fake.*

"Why'd you say you don't know how to kiss?"

Her cheeks darkened into a shade closer to red, but she met his gaze, attempting and failing at looking regal. "Because I *don't*. My brothers didn't exactly let me out of the compound to *date*, and then I was, you know, kidnapped by a psycho who wouldn't touch me because my belly button wasn't symmetrical."

"Your belly button wasn't... What?"

But she was bulldozing on. "So, I haven't exactly been kissed or anything else, thank you very much."

"You've been free two years." Which he shouldn't have pointed out, nor should he continue this line of conversation, or step even closer.

But he did. Stepped closer and continued.

Her eyes were wide and dark and on him like she couldn't quite force herself to look away. "I... I... I've been building a business," she said, her voice something like a squeak. "And a f-family of sorts, and I... Guys aren't really impressed when you can kick their ass."

His mouth curved. "I don't think you could kick my ass, but you can try if you'd like."

"Bennet," she said so seriously he held his breath, afraid to speak and ruin the moment when her eyes held his and she looked like she was going to confess the world.

Or move in for a real kiss.

"I can't go to a ball," she said in that same serious, grave tone. "Look at me."

His breath whooshed out and he cursed himself for an idiot. She was not going to kiss him, and he should hardly want her to. She was innocent on every level and involved with the most important case of his life.

He needed to get himself together. Focus. Channel a little all-business Vaughn Cooper. "Admittedly your current look is a little bedraggled, but I can fix that."

"*You* can fix that?"

"Well, my staff can make you blend right in."

She folded her arms over her chest and scowled at him skeptically, but he noticed she stopped arguing.

"The ball will be attended by a variety of my mother's political supporters and donors, which means the possibility of Sal Cochrane being there is high. I need you there, on the off chance you recognize him or something about him. I'll need an extra set of eyes who knows at least enough about the Jimenez and Dominguez cartels to notice something that might connect. You're integral, Alyssa."

She seemed to consider that very hard and then finally rolled her eyes. "Fine."

Bennet grinned. "Who knows, you might even enjoy it."

WHEN ALYSSA WOKE the next morning, it was with her cheek stuck to a variety of printouts Bennet had given her last night to pore over. She yawned, peeling the paper off her face. She'd dozed off before finishing the read-through.

But lists of people she'd never heard of and the kind of money they handed over to Bennet's parents for political crap was not exactly tantalizing reading. She'd much prefer criminal records or something with a little pizazz.

She stretched out on the big bed and sighed. Oh, a

girl could get used to this kind of luxury. She'd had nice things growing up, even if she had been kept mostly locked up and away, but between two years with The Stallion and two years on her own, luxury had been sorely missing from her life.

But this was a luxury borne of the investigation into her mother's murder. Which caused her to think about last night. A few too many things about last night, but mostly Bennet saying she deserved justice, too.

She was afraid of how much that disarmed her. How much all those little touches that seemed to come so easy to him—an elbow touch, wiping tears off her cheeks—kept throwing her off balance, changing something.

Alyssa blew out a breath. She had to find some kind of power against him. Something to shield herself from all that charm and random acts of sweetness or saying things that felt like soul-deep truths.

Justice. For both of you.

Her life had been unfair, and she knew dwelling on that would send her spiraling into the same awful mental space she'd been in when she'd been kidnapped by The Stallion, but justice had been a foreign concept. The fact it no longer was, the fact someone wanted to fight for her own justice was... Overwhelming. Scary.

Irresistible. And she'd never had to resist anything before. There'd been nothing to resist. She'd only ever wanted freedom, and she'd been given it at twenty-two and somehow created her own little box to exist in.

But all her boxes were colliding, and she didn't know what to do with that. Unfortunately, staying in his comfortable bed was not an option. Something had to be done, and…

She stared hard at the ceiling above her. Bennet had said he needed her. Her help. Her brain. No one had ever needed her before. Gabby had been the first person in her whole life to ask her for help, but Gabby had always been the clear leader in the kidnapping house. Alyssa had followed, had helped, but Gabby hadn't needed her. Not really.

Bennet used the word *need*. Repeatedly. It filled her with hope and fear and a million other things she didn't know what to do with, but the possible only positive of living in basic captivity was that she'd learned to deal with just about anything.

All you could do was keep going.

She slid out of bed and went to pull on her jeans, but noticed that just inside the door was a stool with a pile of neatly folded clothes. She frowned, uncomfortable that she'd slept through someone putting something in her room.

She peered at the stack and noticed a note on top. *Amazing what staff can do. Should fit well enough.*

She scowled at the note and then the stack of clothes. Arrogant man. Still, it *would* be nice to put on some clean clothes. Of course, it reminded her she still hadn't visited Natalie in the hospital. They were probably going home today.

Alyssa shook her head as she got dressed. She had to do what she had to do, and with Oscar clearly knowing where she was and how to get inside without tipping any security off, Alyssa had to be careful. She couldn't bring Natalie and Gabby into this.

So, she grabbed her phone and texted her most sincere apologies to both women. She'd make it up to them, explain everything, she just had to make sure she was out of danger first.

And if you're never out of danger?

A question for another day. She headed for the kitchen, where she had no doubt she'd find Bennet hunched over his computer.

"You're terribly predictable, Ranger Stevens," she offered in greeting, heading for the coffee. She was going to get used to the stuff if it killed her. "How's your back?"

"Sal Cochrane does not exist," Bennet said, ignoring her question.

"What?"

"I have been through every lawful search I can make on that name, every spelling, everything. There is no Sal Cochrane in Austin, Texas. And expanding the search doesn't give me any leads either."

"Maybe he doesn't live in Texas."

"Maybe, but why would someone who doesn't live in Texas donate anything to my mother's campaign? She's a state senator."

"Well, that's if we're working under the assumption Sal Cochrane is on the up-and-up." She felt bad bringing it up, because it implicated his icy mother, but still. It was true. "I could ask Jaime for help. He might have access to some different searches than you guys do, or maybe the name has been involved in an FBI investigation or two."

His face blanked. "We're not bringing in the FBI."

"Not even just for information?"

"It's never just information with the FBI, Alyssa."

Which was maybe true, but it didn't help them any. She wanted to argue with him, but she'd figured enough out about Bennet that arguing only made him dig his heels in deeper. She could always contact Jaime herself, ask for any information he could give without the FBI getting involved, but she didn't think lying to Bennet would go over well. Especially after she'd kept the Oscar thing from him, no matter how briefly.

"I emailed my father's assistant for a list of Mom's campaign donors, along with the guest list of the ball. Maybe that'll give us something to go on."

"Why did you email your father's assistant for information about your mother's campaign donors?"

Bennet smiled wryly. "Because if my mother got wind of my asking her assistant for anything, the barrage of questions I would be piled under would make a criminal interrogation look like a walk in the park. Dad already knows I'm nosing around, so it made sense to go through his people."

"And he won't tell your mother?"

"I believe he'd also like to avoid the interrogation." Something on his computer pinged. "There it is." He gestured for her to come next to him where she could see the screen, too.

He opened one of the email attachments, and they both started scanning it.

"There," Alyssa said, pointing at the name. "S. Cochrane."

"S. Cochrane. SCD Enterprises LLC," Bennet muttered. "That sounds like a front company if I ever heard one."

"A front for what?"

"Anything. Money laundering. Drugs."

"A cartel?"

He sucked in a breath, let it out. "It could be."

Which meant his mother might be connected to cartel business. "Bennet—"

"I don't suppose those names mean anything to you or what you know about your family's business."

"I wouldn't know anything about actual business. I sometimes overheard names or connections, but nothing official like this."

"All right, well, I'll start doing some searching on this LLC and we'll see what I find, but first…" He pulled up the other document, the guest list for the Stevens Christmas Gala.

"He's on the guest list." Bennet nodded firmly. "That's good. That's very good."

Alyssa studied him. He was all tense muscles and

clenched jaw and steely gaze today. No charming smiles, no little insinuations over how close they were standing. He wanted to pretend this was all business, but it wasn't. It was family, too.

"If you did turn this over to the FBI, you wouldn't have to be the one who—"

His cutting blue gaze stopped her dead.

"If my mother is knowingly involved in something illegal," he began firmly and forcefully, "then it is my duty and my right to bring her to justice."

"It isn't always that easy."

He stood abruptly from the table. "For me, it is." He stalked over to the coffeepot and Alyssa glanced at the guest list. For a second, it felt as though her heart had stopped.

"Bennet?"

"Please don't try to argue—"

"My father is on the guest list."

Chapter Nine

Bennet stared at the name he hadn't paid any attention to. Carlos Jimenez.

"My parents did not invite a known drug cartel kingpin to our Christmas gala. The press would crucify them both. This is insanity." In no world would his parents invite *Carlos Jimenez* to their Christmas gala. Good lord.

"Bennet…"

"It's a mistake of some kind. A different Carlos Jimenez. Some horrible prank by a political opponent."

"Bennet."

He glanced at her then instead of the completely insane name on his computer screen. She was pale, hugging herself, wide-eyed.

"What is it? You're not going to have to see him. It can't be true."

"I know it isn't true. Bennet, my father… He isn't well. Mentally or physically. CJ runs everything now. He couldn't possibly come even if he wanted to."

Bennet tried to process that, *understand* it. The FBI, the Rangers and probably half of the Austin police department were trying to find Carlos Jimenez, and he wasn't *well*.

"This is bad. This is wrong and bad and..." She looked up at him, looking as scared as he'd ever seen her. Which, per usual when it came to Alyssa, didn't make any damn sense.

"It's got to be some other Carlos Jimenez. That's a common enough name. It's just a coincidence."

"It's not a coincidence. It's a warning. It's... Something is very, very wrong here. There aren't coincidences right now."

"We'll go to the gala and find out ourselves. Whatever's wrong, whatever's weird, we have the upper hand."

"How?"

"We're on the right side."

She laughed bitterly. "Oh, you are Superman, without the invincibility. Right is not an upper hand. Nothing is an upper hand with all this. CJ is screwing with us, and maybe not just CJ. We don't know who all is involved, and this... Something is very, very wrong, Bennet."

"Yes, we have some question marks, but that's the point. We have to find out, and if we do it right, we will. We'll find out and we'll bring them down."

"Or they kill us, Bennet. Because they can."

She was exhausting. Every time he thought he'd gotten through to her she backed away. Got scared.

"How do you ever track down a skip with this kind of attitude?"

"I'm not tracking down a skip. I'm trying to keep myself and the people I care about *safe*. I'd been safe for two whole years until you showed up."

"So, you're blaming me?"

She raked her hands through her hair. "No!"

"Do you want to stop?" he demanded.

"I…"

"Because we can stop. We can name the Jane Doe, call the case cold, leave it all alone. The end. There are plenty of other cold cases I can work on. Your brother and whoever else was involved in your mother's murder and *your* kidnapping can go along doing whatever they're doing. Justice can just die here, if that's what you really want."

"Oh, screw you," she muttered, and stalked out of the kitchen.

Which he'd take as a no, that's not what she wanted. She wanted justice just as much as he did. More, maybe. She was scared, clearly, though it surprised him. She'd described an awful childhood, a terrible ordeal being kidnapped for *years*, was an illegal bounty hunter for Pete's sake, and yet she was running scared. Constantly.

Something didn't add up, and he didn't like that. She'd promised him she'd told him everything, and he needed to be able to trust her. How could he do that—

An odd noise broke through the silence. Bennet

frowned and listened. Silence. Well, maybe Alyssa had just stomped or punched a wall or something. She *was* quite pissed.

Something else, a squeak or a groan or… The back of his neck prickled with foreboding, and maybe he was overreacting, but in the current state of things it didn't hurt to check out a little overreaction.

He moved down the hall silently, listening for any more sounds. Silence, silence, then something that sounded like a bump. Alyssa was probably just stomping around her room, but…

Bennet curled his fingers around the butt of his gun in the holster on his hip as he approached Alyssa's room. She'd probably laugh at him, but maybe she'd stop being so scared if she laughed at him.

He eased the door open, and Alyssa was standing by the window.

"Oh, good. I thought I—"

The distinct sound of a safety clicking off and the cold press of metal to his temple pissed him off. Not nearly as much as the drop of blood trailing down Alyssa's cheek from her temple.

"Keep your head forward and drop any weapons and kick them behind you," the man with the gun whispered. "You try anything, I kill you both."

"Oh, come on now. You're not going to hurt your sister."

"You think I'm Jimenez? Insulting."

The gun dug harder into Bennet's temple, and he'd admit there was a little fear now. Was this really not one of her brothers? That couldn't be good, but it *did* mean they were moving in the right direction.

"Drop the weapons."

Bennet forced himself to remain calm, to carefully pull his weapon from its holster. Jumping out of the way or swinging the gun at this man was too dangerous. He would fire off a shot one way or another, and it could hit Alyssa.

So, Bennet had to worry about disarming him before he worried about weapons. He set the gun on the ground, gently nudged it behind him as he held up one finger at his side where the man couldn't see him, then held up two, adding his best questioning eyebrow, hoping Alyssa understood his code.

She lifted her bound hands to the wound this man must have inflicted on her, and would pay for. Bloodily. But as she dropped her hand, she held up one single finger.

One he could take.

"On your knees," the man demanded, jabbing the gun harder against his head again.

"Just don't shoot," Bennet said, trying to inflict his voice with some fear, even though the last thing he was was afraid. He was furious.

"No use fighting, idiot. I'm taking her, and if you try to stop me, you will die. Maybe not today, but soon, and painfully, and in a way no one will ever find your body. Do we understand each other?"

"Perfectly," Bennet replied, and before he'd even

gotten the word out he struck, landing a tight-fisted blow to the man's throat.

The gun went off at almost the exact time Alyssa launched herself across the room and against her assailant. The man fell and Bennet flung himself on top of the assailant, who'd fallen to the ground at Alyssa's attack, ignoring the pinpricks of pain in his back from yesterday's wounds. The attacker fought viciously, kicking and nearly landing an unmanning blow before Bennet had him pinned to the ground. But pinning him meant he didn't have any limbs left to inflict a blow.

He glanced up at Alyssa. "Break his nose."

"Gladly." And with perfect form, even with her hands bound together, Alyssa jabbed her elbow into the man's nose with a sickening crack and a satisfying spurt of blood.

The man screamed in pain, and Bennet used the distraction to shift enough so he could roll the man onto his stomach, using his knee to hold him down while he jerked the man's arms behind his back roughly.

"I think he has more zip ties in his pocket," Alyssa said, nodding behind her back.

This man had broken into his home, restrained and hurt Alyssa, and he had *more* zip ties in his pocket. Bennet dug his knee harder into the man's back. "Kneel on his hands."

"Oh… I… Okay." Alyssa shuffled one way and

then the other before lowering into a kneeling position on the back of their assailant.

"Really dig your knees into his wrists so he can't move, and I'll grab the zip ties."

The man groaned in agony, and Bennet flashed a grin. "Good girl." With absolutely no finesse, he roughly searched the man's pockets until he found the zip ties. He gave Alyssa a boost back to her feet then as roughly and tightly as he could, he connected the ties around the man's wrists and ankles.

Bennet stood and watched as the man writhed and groaned. Bennet was tempted to kick him for good measure, but Alyssa still had her hands bound and he wanted to get her freed as soon as possible.

"Where's your knife?"

She cleared her throat. "Well, it's where it always is."

"Which pocket?"

"Um… Well…"

"Where, Alyssa?"

She met his gaze, something indecipherable on her face. "My bra." She bent her elbows, clearly trying to maneuver her fingers into her shirt, but she couldn't bend her elbows or twist her fingers enough to fish it out.

Bennet forced himself to look away from her attempts. "I'll just go get the, uh, kitchen scissors."

Alyssa rolled her eyes. "And leave him here? Just pull it out of my bra, for heaven's sake."

Bennet laughed, couldn't help himself. "And here I thought this job couldn't surprise me any more."

ALYSSA'S TEMPLE THROBBED from where it had hit the bed after the strange man had pushed her down after she'd stepped inside her room. She had no idea where he'd come from, since she'd kept the window locked ever since Oscar had snuck in that way.

She was furious, just righteously livid, that this man had caught her so off guard he'd managed to knock her down and tie her hands. When he'd heard Bennet's approach, he'd jerked her to her feet and told her to stand by the window without saying a word.

She would have told him to take a flying leap, but she hadn't wanted to risk Bennet's life, and she'd trusted that Bennet could get them out of this, and he had. Not just gotten them out of it, but let her break her attacker's nose.

It felt good. It felt like teamwork.

Now Bennet Stevens, Texas Ranger, one hundred tons too charming for his own good, was retrieving the knife from her bra like he was afraid of a pair of breasts. *Her* breasts in particular.

"Don't act like you've never gotten to know your way around a woman's underwear before," she muttered, irritated that no matter how nonchalant she tried to act, her skin felt prickly and tight and all too desperate to know what Bennet's fingertips might feel like across her skin.

He let out a sigh, and then his hand was moving inside her shirt. He paused briefly and cleared his throat. "Um…right or left?"

It was her turn to laugh because, dear Lord this was the most ridiculous situation she'd ever found herself in. "Right."

His fingers brushed the outline of her bra, tracing the seam, touching her skin with the rough, blunt tips of his finger. Oh, God. She was dizzy. Which was possibly the head injury, or the fact he was touching the wrong breast.

"I—I meant *my* r-right," she managed to squeak out. "Not your right."

"That would have been helpful to know before feeling up the other one."

Cheeks on fire, Alyssa did her best to scowl. "You'll live." She knew without a shadow of a doubt she should keep her gaze on the floor, or look up at the ceiling, or even at the bad guy writhing around on the floor, but her gaze drifted to Bennet's.

Who was smiling, all lazy, Texas charm. "Yes, I do believe I will live," he murmured, pulling the Swiss Army knife out of her bra and shirt. "Now, hold out your wrists so I can cut those off."

"What are we going to do with him?"

Bennet stared icily at their attacker. "We're going to leave him here for the time being."

"Here?"

Bennet carefully pulled the knife against the plastic of the zip ties until they snapped, freeing her hands. Then he bent over and retrieved the man's gun and handed it to her. "Keep this on him. He so much as moves a muscle, you have my permission to shoot. I'll be right back."

"Bennet—"

But he was already gone, striding out of the room and picking up his gun he'd been forced to put down on the way out.

"You'll be a dead woman by week's end," the man hissed.

Alyssa kicked his shin. Hard. Then waited for him to finish howling before she spoke. "But I'm not one yet." He would have had her if not for Bennet, and that was humiliating, but Bennet had been there, and Alyssa was no longer running scared.

No, from here on out every clue that led them closer would only firm her resolve. Someone wanted to murder her like they'd murdered her mother? Well, it would take a damn army. No amount of brothers or her father's name could change that.

Bennet returned with a pair of handcuffs and a roll of duct tape. Whistling something that sounded an awful lot like "We Wish You a Merry Christmas," he handcuffed one of the man's bound hands to the foot of the bed. Then, still whistling, he ripped off a length of duct tape and fastened it over the man's mouth.

Without another word, he stood and took Alyssa's arm and led her out of the room. Once in the hallway, any smiles or humor or whistling stopped. Bennet's face went hard and, if Alyssa wasn't totally bad at reading him, furious.

"Wh-what are we going to do?" she asked, because no matter how she tried to free her arm from his grasp, it was like iron. Leading her through the house and to the door to the garage.

"We're going to get you over to my parents' house. They have much heavier security over there."

"What about him?"

"Once I get you settled, I'm going to call the police and report an attempted burglary, of course."

"You're going to lie to the police?"

He stopped her before they walked out the door, taking her by both elbows and pulling her close. "He was one minute away from kidnapping you, and possibly killing you. This isn't just your brothers anymore, and your safety is paramount. I will do whatever it takes to keep you safe while we solve the case, including lying to the local police. Now, can I count on you to do the same?"

"But—"

"But what if my parents are in on it?" he finished for her, clearly irritated by her line of thought.

Still, she nodded.

"Mother will be at her lunch meeting. Dad is at some charity thing until three. Once I get this situated, you are not leaving my sight until we figure this out, and we won't be going anywhere unarmed."

"I'm always armed."

"More than a Swiss Army knife in your bra."

"So, you're going to follow me to the bathroom? Sleep with me?" Which was possibly not the right wording of her question.

"If I have to," he replied unperturbed, beginning to pull her again. Through the garage and out into the open, one hand on her elbow and the other on his holstered gun. He moved quickly and efficiently, scanning every inch of the landscape as they moved from guesthouse to main house.

"He had to have gotten here somehow. Do you think someone else is out there?"

"Maybe," Bennet said in that cold, detached Texas Ranger tone. "If someone else is, they can't be too close with a vehicle. They'd never get past the gates. But we need to hurry on the chance someone is out there, and make sure they don't come looking for our friend."

Bennet keyed a code into the main house's garage door. Practically silently, it glided open and Bennet moved them inside, closing the garage door behind them.

They stepped into what was some sort of finished basement cellar-type thing—stainless steel deep freezer, matching fridge, a pantry full of canned goods and alcohol and all kinds of nonperishables.

Bennet led her up a staircase, and they stepped out in a kitchen where two people were sitting at a table sipping tea.

Bennet nodded at them. "Mrs. Downy. Kinsey.

Can you make sure no staff enter my room for the next few hours?"

The older-looking woman nodded. "Of course."

Then Alyssa was being led out of the kitchen, down another hall, through another room she couldn't ascertain the use for. Then they were clearly in the main entryway because a giant chandelier glittered above them.

It was like a movie. There was a grand staircase in the middle, all gleaming polished woods decorated with garland and red bows. On the other side of the staircase she could catch a glimpse of what had to be a gigantic tree decorated completely in gold.

But Bennet didn't give her any time to soak it in. He was pulling her up the stairs and down a long hall and into another giant room. This one wasn't white, though. It was a kind of forest green and some kind of tan color. Very woodsy and masculine.

"This is *your* room."

"Well, it was when I lived here. Now you're going to sit tight," he instructed, going through and checking all the windows even though they were on the second story. "Don't leave. Don't move, and on the off chance someone comes in this room, you shoot," he ordered, pointing at the gun he'd handed her earlier.

Alyssa frowned at the weapon she held. "What if it's someone from your parents' staff?"

"You heard me leave instructions for no one to

enter. So, if someone does, you can almost be certain it's nefarious."

And clearly she wasn't as smart as she'd always fancied herself to be because she finally understood what was happening. "So, I'm just supposed to sit here in this room? Locked up."

Bennet didn't even pause, already striding for the door. "It's for your own protection, Alyssa."

"That's what they said, too."

He stopped and turned, frowning at her in that way she might have been intimidated by if she wasn't so irrationally hurt by all this.

"It isn't fair to compare me to your brothers."

"Isn't it?" she returned, shrugging as if she didn't have a care in the world.

"I don't have time for this," he muttered, raking a hand through his hair, but he didn't walk out. "I can't have you call the police because then you have to explain why you're in my parents' guesthouse. It's too complicated. You can't go milling around the house because I don't know who in this house we can trust. I actually don't know who we can trust, period, and neither do you. This is temporary while I deal with the police, and I need you on board."

"You need me to sit down and shut up."

"Hey, I let you break that guy's nose. Never accuse me of not using your unique talents." He smiled, but she couldn't bring herself to smile back. This was all too familiar, all too…much. She couldn't stand the idea that she'd felt like Bennet's partner there for a little bit, and now he was going to lock her away, too.

"Alyssa, I can't imagine what this might feel like from your perspective, but try to think about it from mine, okay? I'll be back." And then he was gone and the door was locked. End of discussion.

Alyssa sat down on the bed, fury and hurt pumping through her. But the worst part was knowing he was right and that she had to, once again, sit in a locked room and twiddle her thumbs.

Chapter Ten

Bennet dealt with the police, half his mind elsewhere. He wanted the squad car gone before either of his parents returned home, and he wanted to get back to Alyssa ASAP.

Everything had gotten completely out of hand, and he was half-tempted to send the whole of the Texas Rangers after CJ Jimenez.

But it wouldn't solve his case, and it wouldn't help Alyssa.

Luckily, being a Ranger himself helped speed up the Austin police investigation, and by the time Bennet was allowed to go, they even had a suspected partner in crime and vehicle for the getaway car.

He didn't know who'd sent the men, though, and that was a problem. All of this was an increasingly complicated problem. Bennet grabbed his laptop, his extra sidearm, all the clothes he'd gotten for Alyssa and shoved everything into a bag.

He didn't like the idea of staying at the main house whether his parents were involved in this mess or not, but he couldn't think of a safer place for them right now. Security was tight, and if one of his parents turned out to be his enemy, he'd keep them close and smoke them out.

That was something he couldn't allow himself to think too deeply on. Whatever happened, whatever *justice* was, he'd deal with the emotional fallout when it was over.

He entered through the garage again. When he got to the kitchen, Kinsey was still there, though she was no longer sipping tea with Mrs. Downy, who was in charge of the kitchen. Kinsey was sitting at the table, alone, a computer in front of her.

She'd run this house like a military institution since Bennet could remember, so when she gestured for him to approach, Bennet could only obey.

"Shall I tell your mother you and a guest will be staying with us?"

"You haven't yet?"

Kinsey's mouth curved just a fraction, but Bennet had known the severe woman most of his life. Which meant he knew that smile was a feat indeed, just like when he was a teenager and she'd finally allowed him to call her Kinsey instead of Ms. Kinsey.

"The girl was bleeding. Police cars. I don't want to be the one to break all that to your mother."

"Then don't."

"Someone will."

"*I* will." At least that way he could control the information, gauge his mother's reaction. Did she know? Was she part of this? He hated having doubts about his own parents. No matter how little he got along with them, they were still his family. He loved them.

And it was looking more and more likely one of them had cartel ties.

Kinsey pushed a small box toward him. "Clean her up first."

Damn. He'd been so worked up about getting the attacker and police taken care of, he'd forgotten all about Alyssa's head wound.

"She's pretty," Kinsey commented as Bennet took the box.

"She's work," he replied firmly.

Kinsey made a noncommittal sound that Bennet didn't have time to argue with. He strode through the house and to his room. He knocked, offering his name.

The door unlocked and opened a crack, the barrel of the gun the only thing appearing in the crack.

"Alyssa."

"Just making sure." The door opened the rest of the way, and she was smirking, gun still in her hand. It should not arouse him in the least.

"Uh-huh."

Alyssa set the gun down on the nightstand once he'd entered and closed and locked the door behind him.

"So, what happened?"

"They arrested the guy for breaking and entering and attempted burglary. They think they have a lead on the car that was waiting for him outside the gates. Did you recognize our guy?"

She shook her head. "I tried to pay attention to anything that might have been familiar or connect to anything, but he was nobody I've ever met."

"What about this man?" Bennet asked, pulling out his phone and bringing up the pictures he'd had the Austin officer send him. "He's our suspect for being the driver of the getaway car."

Alyssa frowned, leaning closer to the screen. "He looks familiar. He... He used to work for my father."

"Used to?"

"Yeah. Eli... I don't know last names, or even if that's his real name, but his name was Eli and he worked my father, but he defected." She looked up at him. "I'm sure of it."

"What exactly does *defected* mean?"

"I'm not sure of the exact cartel meaning. I used to think it was going to the cops, but it's what my brothers said about my mom. She defected. To a cartel rival. And if we put it together with what my father told me about Dominguez having my mother... Maybe that's the connection."

"Except we don't know what Dominguez has to do with any of this."

Alyssa swallowed, and though she was trying to look tough, to act tough, he could see the worry in her eyes. "He wants me, though. For whatever reason, he's after me."

"Why now? You've been free for two years. If he wanted you as revenge, he's had years to do it."

"There has to be an inciting incident we don't know about."

"That started recently, but before I came to your office, if your brothers' men were following you on your last job."

"But… I don't know what it would be."

"We'll start looking into cartel cases and see if we can't find some recent dustup we might make a connection to."

"And if we can't?"

Bennet didn't know what to say to that. He was tempted to make a joke about crossing bridges once they were burning behind them, but she didn't look like she'd laugh. Or smile. Or do anything except maybe break.

He couldn't bear the thought of breaking her.

"I don't want to be a prisoner anymore, Bennet. Not one of my family, or a madman, or whatever the hell is going on here. I don't want to be locked up and shoved away. I won't live like that, even if it puts me in danger. I'd rather be dead."

"You're not going to end up dead. Not on my watch."

"What do you care? I shouldn't be anyone to you."

It was such a vulnerable statement, clearly speaking to all those hurts she'd somehow survived. Trust broken over and over again.

He didn't know what it was like to be a prisoner,

not in any sense of the word. Even in the world his parents had created he'd broken mostly free. Maybe they'd greased some palms for him that he'd wished they hadn't, but it was hardly kidnapping or betrayal.

But somehow, despite his complete lack of experience in the matter, he could feel that pain of hers, and he wanted to soothe it. He wanted to be as honest as she was being when he should be cagey or stone-faced or whatever would best benefit this case.

But as gung-ho as he'd been just days ago about solving *this* case, the oldest cold case on file at the Texas Rangers, it had irrevocably become about something else. About her.

"What do I care?" He shook his head. "You hold your own. You make me laugh at the wrongest of times. You're smart, and we understand each other. Justice. We understand that. Not everyone does. Maybe you shouldn't be anyone to me, but you are."

He stepped forward and more than anything else he'd ever wanted in his whole life, he wanted to press his mouth to hers. Not in some ploy to convince his father to leave, or just because he wondered what it might be like. No, he wanted to kiss her because she was her and he thought somehow their mouths fitting together would make everything all right.

But it wouldn't. So, he held up the first aid box Kinsey had given him. "Now, it's my turn to bandage you up."

ALYSSA HATED PORING over paperwork. It was boring. As much as she often had to do some investigating when she was hunting down a skip, she at least got to do stuff. Call people. Go places. Plan.

This was all looking for some magical clue, one that could be absolutely anything. She glanced at Bennet, who was sitting on the window seat, legs stretched out in front of him and crossed at the ankles, focus lasered on the computer screen in front of him. He didn't lean against the wall, likely because of his cuts, but he still looked…powerful and smart and a million other things she should ignore.

Anytime he found something he thought might be important or relevant, he printed it out and made her read it.

She wanted to be useful, but she also wanted to make a move. She'd already learned that being kidnapped with someone wasn't all that much different from being kidnapped alone. In The Stallion's house, there'd been three other girls with her, but it hadn't changed the fact she'd been alone and shut in.

"You can go to bed if you're tired," Bennet offered, never taking his gaze off the screen.

"I'm not tired," Alyssa muttered, poking at the tray of food an older woman had brought up a few hours ago. "I'm bored."

"You'd make a terrible policeman."

"Why do you think I'm a bounty hunter?"

He glanced over at her, mouth curved at one side. "Illegal bounty hunter."

She flashed him a grin. "Even better. Don't have to worry about following any pesky laws."

"How's your head?"

"How's your back?"

"Fine. How's your head?" he repeated, clearly un-amused by her unwillingness to answer the question.

"You should see the other guy."

"I believe I did. Impressive indeed. Seriously, though?"

"It's fine." If fine was painful throbbing. "Didn't even lose consciousness."

"Look, we'll have to sleep in shifts, so you might as well try to grab a few hours."

"Why do we have to sleep in shifts?"

"Well, for starters I'm not going to sleep on the floor."

She cocked her head. She'd sort of assumed she'd sleep on that cushy window seat he was on. He was too tall to fit, but she'd be able to stretch out just fine. It was a little interesting he hadn't thought of that, though. He'd gone straight to the only option being him sleeping on the floor.

Apparently with her was not an option. *You know it's not.* And it shouldn't be something she was imagining. She needed to focus on reality. "You don't think we're safe."

"I don't *know* if we're safe. For the time being, one of us is always on guard. We sleep in shifts. And, while one is sleeping, the other one is working. Until we get to the bottom of it."

Alyssa flopped back on the bed, frowning. "And how am I supposed to sleep with all the lights blazing?"

Without Bennet even moving from the window seat, the lights flicked off.

"Your computer—"

He made a move with his arm without even looking and suddenly he was pulling a curtain from behind him to enclose the little window seat alcove. The room was completely dark.

"Good night, Alyssa," he said from behind the curtain.

Since it was dark and he was behind a curtain, she indulged in the childish impulse to stick her tongue out at him.

"It's too quiet in here," she grumbled.

"No, it isn't, because you keep whining."

She scowled and shifted deeper into the unbelievably soft sheets. She wasn't tired in the least, but she also wasn't *whining*. She was going insane. The walls were closing in, and at least complaining kept them at bay for a while.

How could she sleep when she was locked up again? Oh, this was by far the nicest room she'd been locked in, but amenities didn't matter when you were essentially a prisoner. Hands tied from *doing* anything because they didn't know what the hell was going on.

She scowled over at the curtain Bennet was behind. The irritating thing was she understood why they had to do all this. She just hated it. Hated feeling locked up and ineffective. She wanted to do something. Even if it meant smashing her elbow into some assailant's nose.

At least that had been action. At least that had *felt* good. She wanted something that felt good instead of dark and oppressive. Instead of like her life would only ever be some terrible, lonely prison.

But she wasn't exactly alone right now, curtain or no curtain. Her mind drifted to her kiss with Bennet. *Fake kiss.* Except no matter how the pretense had been fake, the kiss hadn't been. His mouth had been on hers, and more than once his hands had been on her.

Sometimes he looked at her and she was almost certain that whatever she'd felt in the midst of that fake kiss—attraction and need and the desperate curiosity of what more he could do with that all-too-charming mouth of his—he felt it, too.

She didn't know *why* he'd be attracted to someone like her, and she realized she probably wasn't the world's leading expert in men and attraction, but she also wasn't stupid. He'd gently bandaged her head, but on occasion his gaze had drifted to her mouth.

That meant something. She'd spent the past two years in the orbit of Gabby and Jaime, who couldn't seem to keep their hands off each other no matter how committed they got. So, she may not have experience with attraction or lust or anything, but she did know what it looked like.

She'd really like to know what it *felt* like. She'd spent the past two years building something of a free life, but she hadn't dated or flirted or even put herself out there in any way, shape or form because she'd been waiting for something to come to her.

Like all her life she'd waited for freedom. What a waste all that waiting was.

"Bennet?" she asked into the quiet of the room.

"What?"

"How many women have you kissed?"

He made a sound, something like a cough or rough inhale. "I... How is that relevant to anything?"

"I didn't say I was going to ask you a *relevant* question. I'm just asking you *a* question."

He cleared his throat. "I... I don't know. I don't have a running tally."

"Oh? That many." And on some level she wanted to know everything about them. Why he'd kissed them. How far it had gone. What he'd felt.

And on some level she wanted to elbow every woman in the nose just as she'd done to the man who'd attacked her.

"It isn't about how many, it's just... I'd have to do the math and... Why are you asking me this?"

"Well, you know, I've only kissed you."

There was a moment of heavy silence. "That wasn't a kiss," he said, his voice something closer to a growl.

"Oh? What was it then?"

"A…charade."

"A *charade*," she repeated, because even though it had been an act, a fake, *charade* seemed such an oddly proper word.

"That's what I said."

"But I was just thinking if I'm going to die—"

He jerked the curtain open, the harsh computer light glinting off the angry expression on his face. "You're not going to die."

"You can't *promise* I'm not going to die, and God knows someday I will. So. You know. I should probably know what it's like."

"What what's like?"

"Sex."

He didn't move, didn't speak, and she was almost certain he didn't even breathe. Which was kind of funny, all in all. That it just took the mention of sex to catch Ranger Stevens off guard.

And since he was off guard, she slid out of bed and walked over to him. He watched her approach warily, but he didn't ward her off, and he didn't tell her to stop. She walked all the way until her knees were all but touching the window seat. She looked down at him.

He held her gaze, but he still didn't say anything. Everything she knew about Bennet suggested he'd be the kind of man who'd make the first move, and yet he just *sat* there. Not making *any* move.

"It would be something of a no-no, wouldn't it?"

she asked, her voice a little breathless with some-thing like nerves but not quite that. Adrenaline, maybe. *Anticipation.* "Because I'm involved in this case."

"First of all, please never say the phrase 'no-no' again. Second of all, yes. It would be incredibly wrong. On every level."

"Come on. Not *every* level."

"Okay, nine out of ten levels," he returned, and she could tell he was trying very hard not to be amused.

"So, maybe we explore that one-out-of-ten level," Alyssa offered hopefully, covertly moving to take the computer off his lap. Except as she glanced at the screen she noticed something oddly familiar. Some-thing she hadn't seen in years.

"What is this a picture of?" she asked breath-lessly, this time not nerves or anticipation or any-thing other than the excitement they might find a lead.

"What... What?" Bennet asked, clearly not mak-ing the leap to work quite as quickly as she had.

"The picture you have on the screen," she said, pointing at it as she leaned in closer. "What's it of?"

"Uh... I... The FBI believes the man on the right is Salvador Dominguez. It's the only known picture of him law enforcement has as far as I know."

"And the man next to him?"

"No one's identified him. It's too shadowy, he's

looking away from the camera and there're no markings to give any clues."

"But there is an earring."

Bennet squinted at the screen. "I suppose."

"It's one of my brothers."

His head jerked toward hers. "How do you know that?"

"The earring. It's a *J* with dragon horns. It was my father's. Now, that definitely isn't my father. This guy is too tall, too broad. But it's one of my brothers, I can almost guarantee it. My father wouldn't have given that earring to anyone else. When was this photo taken?"

"Last month."

"So, one of my brothers is photographed talking with the head of a rival cartel a month ago."

Bennet blew out a breath. "Well, it looks like we might have our inciting incident, doesn't it?"

"I don't know what *I* have to do with it, though."

"Your brothers love you. To bad men trying to hurt each other, love is a weapon. A weakness."

She glanced at Bennet, feeling unaccountably sad for some reason. "That isn't just to bad men trying to hurt each other, Bennet. Love is always a weapon."

"It doesn't have to be," he replied steadfastly, his blue eyes an odd shade in the light of the laptop screen.

Her chest felt tight, and her heart felt too much like it was being squeezed. She'd wanted to feel something, but not this. Not anything to do with love, especially when it came to her brothers. *If* they loved her, that love had only ever been used as a weapon, no matter what Bennet thought.

"Well, I guess we've got something to go on now," she said, straightening and wrapping her arms around herself. She felt sad and alone and suddenly she wouldn't mind just going to bed and being locked away. "I'll take my sleeping shift, then."

Before she realized what he was doing, Bennet had his hand fisted in her shirt and jerked her down so that she had to grab his shoulders or risk just falling into his lap.

Then his mouth was on hers. Gentle, and something that kind of made her want to cry because there'd been so little of it in her life. Softness. His lips caressed hers, his tongue slowly tracing the outline of her bottom lip, and all she could do was soak it up.

She felt like melted wax and a firework ready to burst all at the same time, and underneath her hands his shoulders were just these steady rocks to lean on.

He pulled away, though his hand was still fisted in her shirt, and his breath wafted across her still-wet lips.

"*That* was a kiss," he murmured. He released her and grabbed the curtain. "Now go to sleep," he ordered, and snapped the curtain closed between them.

Chapter Eleven

Bennet woke with a start and then a groan of pain. He'd dozed off on the stupid window seat and now his neck and shoulders were paying the price, the cuts on his back throbbing. He rubbed his eyes, realizing through the gauzy fabric of the curtains that covered the window, daylight shone far brighter than he'd have liked.

He should have been up hours ago. He should have never fallen asleep. Sleep was wasting precious time they didn't have to unravel all of these confusing clues.

He fumbled for the curtain that separated the window seat from the room and managed to shove it open.

Alyssa was sitting in the bed, cross-legged with his laptop perched on her thighs. There was a tray of fresh fruit and bagels and a coffeepot on the bed next to her.

"How'd you get that?"

"Ms. Kinsey brought up the food and coffee—

much better than yours, FYI. The laptop? I took it while you snored away. Very unattractive, I might add."

Bennet grunted irritably, remembering exactly why he'd allowed himself to doze off on the window seat.

The thought of waking up Alyssa, asleep in his bed, warm and soft and more alluring than she had any right to be, had been a little too much to bear at two in the morning. He'd been afraid that if he'd even simply nudged her shoulder he'd want to touch all of her.

And that was most wholeheartedly a *no-no*. Which made kissing her last night inexcusable and irrational and something he had no business considering in the light of the morning.

"Coffee?" she asked sweetly.

"Are you always this obnoxious in the morning?"

"Morning is the absolute best time of day."

He grabbed the coffeepot and one of the mugs and poured. "You're evil."

She laughed, and no matter how much he hated mornings or the awful, digging pain in his neck and the fact his back felt like it was on fire, he liked hearing her laugh. He liked a few too many things about Alyssa Jimenez, drug kingpin's daughter.

Yeah, that was never going to fly in any of his lives—Texas Ranger, politicians' son. The conclusion of this case would be the conclusion of their time together.

You can't promise I'm not going to die, and God knows someday I will. So. You know. I should probably know what it's like.

Those words kept bouncing around in his brain, completely unwelcome. Someday she *would* know what it was like, but it wouldn't be with him. For all the reasons he'd gone through a million times over.

"Find anything?" he asked, easing onto the other side of the bed, enough space and a tray of food between them, to keep his head on the case.

Maybe.

"Well, I found that no matter how hard or zoomed in I look at the picture, I can't tell which of my brothers is in that picture. I have committed Salvador Dominguez's face to memory, though, and I can't help but thinking he's behind yesterday."

"Agreed."

"How did you connect my mother to me when she was a Jane Doe?"

"Happenstance. I was searching old case files and happened to notice a similarity in a murder that was committed by a known member of the Jimenez cartel. The victim in that murder had the exact same wounds and was buried in the exact same way not too far from where…"

She'd looked away, but he understood that thinking of her mother's wounds and where her body was found was too much even for Alyssa.

"What I didn't know when I came to see you was that my Jane Doe *was* a Jimenez."

"Who was the man convicted of the other murder?"

"Dom Coch… Holy hell. Dom Cochrane. Spelled differently, but that's too much of a coincidence to the name your brother gave us."

"I don't remember anyone named Dom, but I wouldn't have known everyone, I guess."

Bennet gestured for her to hand over the laptop. She did so, and he logged into the Ranger system while he sipped his coffee. "I'm going to do some searches for Dom Cochrane and see what pops up."

Alyssa took one of the bagels off the tray between them and spread cream cheese across the top. She frowned at it while Bennet typed the name into the database.

Something was bothering her, and she wasn't saying what. He didn't like knowing she was keeping something from him, even if it was feelings rather than information. He wanted to know everything. About the case. About her.

Which was the absolute last thing he needed right now. He tried to focus on the results of his search, but Alyssa licked a smudge of cream cheese off her thumb. Which he shouldn't watch. Or think about.

Either she felt his gaze or just happened to look over, but somehow their gazes met as her thumb disappeared into her mouth. Everything inside him tightened and ached, and would it really be *that* bad to indulge in something this potent? He'd still solve the case, and maybe it was morally ambiguous to get involved with someone connected to one of his cases, but hell, Vaughn had done it, and he was the most morally upstanding person Bennet had ever met.

A sharp knock sounded at the door, and they both nearly jumped a foot, the tray tipping over and spilling the remaining bagels onto the bed.

"Who is it?" Bennet growled.

"Kinsey."

He shoved the computer off his lap and strode over to the door, doing everything he could to take his mind off the completely untimely erection.

He opened the door a crack. "Yes?"

Kinsey looked vaguely amused, but her message was brief.

"Ms. Delaney is here with the dresses. Shall I send her up here?"

"That would be perfect. Thank you."

Kinsey nodded and Bennet shut the door. He had half a mind to bang his head against it. Instead, he turned back to the bed to find Alyssa staring at him, her eyebrows drawn together.

"You really grew up like this?"

"Like what?"

"Servants? Everything at your beck and call. Dresses... Wait." She sat up straighter on the bed. "What did she say about *dresses*?"

Bennet tried not to smile, but half his mouth curved of its own accord. "You'll need something for the ball."

"But..."

"We can't exactly go to the *mall* after you've been

attacked, so I asked Kinsey what we could do. She suggested calling one of my mother's personal shoppers with your size and have them make a house call."

"B-but… I can't afford…"

"Alyssa, honestly."

"I don't want you paying for stuff," she said stubbornly.

"Except I'm the one *forcing* you to go to this gala, and you'll need to fit in if we have hope of getting any information. Which means jeans and a T-shirt aren't going to cut it, and neither is…well, no offense, darling, but anything you'd pick out on your own."

She scowled at him, which was good. Better her to be angry with him than anything else.

"And, just so you can settle into the idea before Friday night, I'll also be hiring a hair and makeup person to do all that stuff women do."

"What stuff?"

"Hell if I know, but the person I hire will, and that's all that matters. Now, you can pick whatever dress you'd like. Cost is no option."

"Oh, well, then why don't you shower me with jewels, too," she returned sarcastically.

"Don't tempt me."

She opened her mouth, likely to say something scathing, but another knock sounded at the door.

Bennet opened it, smiling at Tawny Delaney, whom he'd met on occasion at events such as the

Christmas gala. Her father was in oil and a dedicated donor to his father's many political endeavors.

Tawny also *might* have been on the list of women he'd kissed, and he couldn't help but be glad Alyssa didn't have any such list.

"Ben. It's so good to see you again," Tawny said, smiling up at him.

"Thank you for coming," he returned, ushering her in. A man with a rolling rack of what Bennet could only assume were dresses began to push the rack inside, but Bennet slapped a palm to the rack.

"I'll take it from here, sir. You can wait down in the foyer, if you'd be so kind."

"Ben?"

"Sorry. Can't be too careful right now."

"Oh. Well. That's fine," Tawny replied, though she looked a little nervous. "Where's our client?"

Bennet gestured to the bed, where Alyssa was sprawled out, defiantly so, scowling. Bennet wanted to laugh even though it was ridiculous.

"Oh, well." Tawny cleared her throat, her smile looking so forced Bennet winced. "Won't this be fun?"

"Yes, it will. Won't it, Alyssa?" he said, giving her a meaningful look he hoped she realized meant *get your butt off the bed.*

"Sure it will, *Ben*," Alyssa said, emphasis on the shortened name, still lounging on the rumpled covers.

It was more than likely he was going to end up paying very dearly for this.

ALYSSA WATCHED AS Tawny the tall, put-together blonde started taking the covers off the dresses on the rack. She chattered on about jewel tones and coloring, and all Alyssa could think was she would never in a million years look like this woman.

There would always be a little drowned sewer rat in her. A girl who'd grown up locked in a room with only men for companions. Even when her mother had been alive and around she hadn't spent much time *around*. The kids were supposed to play with each other while the adults did the serious business of running a cartel.

"Where should we do the trying on?" Tawny asked brightly.

"There's a bathroom through that door there," Bennet offered.

"Perfect." Tawny turned her attention to Alyssa, all bright smiles and comforting drawl. "We'll start with three. More than three and it gets overwhelming." She plucked three dresses off the rack and rested them across her arm before marching for the bathroom. "These are my top choices based on your coloring and build."

She stepped inside the bathroom and waited for Alyssa to hesitantly enter before she closed the door shut and hung the dresses on the shower curtain.

"My, the Stevenses do know how to build a house, don't they?" Tawny said conversationally. She handed Alyssa a blindingly gold dress. "Let's start with this one."

Alyssa recoiled. Visibly. "No."

Tawny blinked, and for a fraction of a second Alyssa felt kind of crappy for her antagonistic behavior. It wasn't this woman's fault she was everything Alyssa wasn't and never could be.

"It's a beautiful dress," Alyssa offered, shoving her hands into her pockets. "It's too loud for this. I need to blend in."

Tawny smiled indulgently. "Isn't it every woman's fantasy to stand out?"

The question landed a little hard, right in the heart. Stand out? All standing out had ever gotten her was locked up, and somehow she still wanted that moment. A moment when the attention was on her for something *good* for once.

But, this wasn't that moment. "This is more a business venture than a personal, womanly venture."

"Okay, well, let's try the black, then." She held out a black dress with a fluffy thing of green hanging off it.

Alyssa wanted to refuse this one, too, but it was no use. She did have to fit in, and fitting in meant some fancy dress the likes of which she'd never even dreamed about wearing it was so foreign to all the lives she'd lived.

She took it and waited for Miss Texas Perfect to leave, but Tawny just waited expectantly.

"Oh, well, I'm supposed to stay with the dresses," Tawny explained. "Part of the job. I do it all the time." Sensing Alyssa's continued hesitation, Tawny nodded. "How about I turn my back?"

"Sure," Alyssa muttered. Maybe it was stupid, but the last thing she wanted was Tawny seeing her sub-par underwear. Tawny probably had a matching set. All silk or lace or something beautiful and expensive.

And what would you ever do with something like that?

Hoping to get it over with as quickly as possible, Alyssa shucked her clothes and roughly pulled on the dress. It was black, somehow fit like a glove, and though she'd probably *never* feel comfortable in a dress, it wasn't scratchy or uncomfortable or anything.

"So, how do you know Ben?" the woman asked conversationally, trailing her perfectly manicured pink nails across the decorative towels hanging off a rack next to the sink.

"Uh. Work," Alyssa muttered, tugging the zipper in the back up as far as she could.

"Oh. Are you a Ranger?" Tawny asked, as if it was somehow possible her scrawny self could be a Ranger.

Alyssa couldn't help but smile. "No. Just…helping out."

"It must be dangerous if you're working with the Rangers. Aren't you scared?"

"Sometimes, but I know how to protect myself."

Tawny sighed. "No wonder Ben likes you. He's

one of the few men I've ever met who wasn't impressed or enthralled by weakness."

Alyssa didn't know *what* to say to that, so she smoothed her hands down the dress. "Uh, I'm done."

Tawny turned and clapped her hands together. "Oh, isn't that perfect!"

Alyssa had her doubts about perfect, but Tawny was immediately fussing, pulling the zipper up the rest of the way, tying the green ribbon around her waist into a beautiful bow Alyssa would never be able to replicate.

Tawny nudged her over to the full-length mirror, forcing Alyssa to look at her reflection.

"You'll want to sweep your hair back, and have someone do your makeup, obviously," Tawny said, pulling Alyssa's hair back herself, artfully brushing some hair to hide the bandage on her forehead. "Maybe a tasteful necklace. Diamonds or rubies. Nothing ostentatious. You'll fit right in without standing too far out."

Even with no makeup and someone else holding her hair back, Alyssa didn't recognize herself. It was like someone had put a fancy filter over the girl she'd always been.

"Do you want Ben's opinion?"

Even though she'd warmed to the woman a little bit, Alyssa still *hated* her calling Bennet Ben. "No. I think I'd like it to be a surprise."

The woman smiled somewhat wistfully. "He isn't an easy man to surprise, but this might do the trick."

"Do you know him well?"

Tawny's smile didn't change. "Sometimes I wonder if anyone knows him well. And for the record, I call him Ben because it irritates him and that's about the only time he'll pay me any mind."

"Oh."

"But you don't seem to have that trouble."

Alyssa turned away from the mirror. This woman was confusing, and Alyssa didn't have any idea how to talk to her. She seemed…well, perfect for Bennet's world of icy mothers and charming fathers and smooth, Southern drawls.

And somehow this tall blonde with class and elegance for miles seemed to be under the impression Bennet liked Alyssa. And that wasn't weird, just something to sigh over.

Alyssa moved back to her regular clothes, and Tawny dutifully turned her back again. "W-why do you think he likes me?" Alyssa couldn't help but ask, pulling the zipper down. "This is all work."

"You're in his bedroom, sweetheart. He might be calling it work, but men are apt to say lots of things to get a woman into their bedroom."

It all sounded so worldly and adult, and Alyssa felt like a child again. A child playing at being an adult.

Except she was twenty-four. And she'd survived what might kill most people. She was not some little girl. She was just a little inexperienced.

But Bennet had kissed her last night. Of his own accord, with no pretending it had been meant to throw anyone off. It had been a *real* kiss. He'd said so himself.

So, it was time. Time to get rid of the inexperience, and if she ended up doing that before they unraveled their myriad of mysteries, well, so be it.

She had a life to live, after all, and she was tired of it being thwarted.

Chapter Twelve

Once Tawny left with the dresses, Bennet made himself scarce. He knew Alyssa wasn't happy with him for running some mysterious errands, but he also knew she was losing her mind locked up in that room. So, he set about a safe way to give her a little excursion.

It wasn't necessary, and it would take time away from the case he was trying to solve, but…

Hell. He hated that wild look in her eyes like she was reliving all the ways she'd been a prisoner in her life. He hated the way she paced that room like it was some kind of cage. And, worst of all, he liked way too much the way she'd sometimes stare at him, considering, assessing. The same look she'd had in her eyes last night when she'd approached him before seeing the picture on his computer and recognized one of her brothers.

One of her brothers. Possibly fraternizing with a rival cartel. A lead, something to go on. What he should be focused on instead of Alyssa's state of mind.

But no matter how he chastised himself for his lack of focus, he still secured his parents' screening room, checking every nook and cranny, locking it down in a way that eased his worries. It was still just another locked room, but it wasn't the room he currently had her locked in.

He had no idea if she'd appreciate it, but it was worth a shot. And she could pick a movie and some snacks and he could still focus on finding a connection between Sal/Dom Cochrane, Salvador Dominguez and one of Alyssa's brothers.

So, he was hardly ignoring his duties or his case. And if he'd told Captain Dean he was taking a vacation until after Christmas even though he was working on this case 24/7, it was only to keep Alyssa safe. It wasn't lying to his superior. It was protecting a vulnerable piece of the case.

He'd work on believing that. He left the movie room, locked sufficiently, and went to collect Alyssa for their little…night in. Not theirs. Hers. It was like a gift.

Certainly not like a date.

He forced that thought out of his head and walked up the stairs, hand on the butt of his weapon, scanning every corner for anything suspicious.

It was strange to walk through his parents' house feeling like danger could be lurking anywhere. He'd grown up in this house and there had been a lot of feelings it had prompted. Suffocating, cold, frustration, disgust. But never fear.

It made him sick to his stomach to think too hard about his mother being involved in this, but if Sal Cochrane was connected to Dom Cochrane, and they were both connected to Salvador Dominguez…

Ambition had made worse monsters out of people. He just hated to believe it of his mother even with as strained a relationship as they had.

But he would find the truth regardless. Justice. One way or another.

He walked down the hall to his room, something uncomfortable jittering in his gut, and it wasn't the fear of danger or worry over his mother's involvement.

It was anticipation and nerves. No one had ever affected him quite like Alyssa did, and he wasn't altogether certain he liked it, but he seemed incapable of resisting it.

He knocked, three hard raps. "It's Bennet."

The door edged open, just a crack. She didn't open it farther, so he pushed in himself.

He made a noise, one he couldn't have described to save his life. Everything just kind of whooshed out of him.

She was standing there in one of his button-down dress shirts. And that was all. Her long legs bare from midthigh on down to her toes. She'd left the top of the shirt unbuttoned far enough he could see the enticing tops of her breasts.

"This is your shirt, right?" she asked, her expression unreadable.

"Uh, yup. That's…my shirt." He glanced around the room and found her jeans and pointed at them. "You should put some pants on."

She cocked her head, toying with the top buttoned button of his shirt. If she undid it…

"Why?"

He'd completely lost his train of thought. "Why what?"

"Why should I put pants on?"

"Oh, right." He cleared his throat, trying to speak past the dryness there. "I have a surprise for you."

She took a few steps toward him, still toying with that button, and no matter how strictly he ordered himself to look away, he simply couldn't. She looked impossibly soft, even knowing how tough and strong she could be.

She reached out, pressing her palm against his chest, looking up at him from underneath her lashes. "Let's do my surprise first."

He should not ask for details on that. He should not be deterred. He should… Hell.

He managed to clear his throat and put his hand over hers, gently pulling it off his chest. "I have a feeling your surprise isn't very…appropriate."

"No, it's very, very inappropriate." She grinned up at him, and he shouldn't smile back, but he couldn't help it.

"Alyssa…"

"Don't say no to the virgin throwing herself at you. That'd scar her for life."

He reached out and touched the edge of the bandage on her head. She hadn't complained about it once. "Nothing I could do would scar you for life."

She stepped closer. This time instead of pressing her palm to his chest, she stood on her toes and wound her arms around his neck. She was all soft curves against him, the fragrance of his own damn soap on her skin and in her hair.

"I want you, Bennet. And you want me, too... I think."

"I do."

"Okay, well, you may have gotten most of the things you've wanted in life, but I've gotten very few. So, it's my turn to get something, have something, I want."

"I thought you wanted to get out of here."

"This'll do." Then her mouth was on his, and what could he do but pull her closer, sink into that kiss. He slid his hands down the sexy curve of her back, exploring her mouth with his tongue. When his hands slid over her ass, he realized she was not, in fact, wearing any underwear.

"Hell."

She laughed against his mouth, pressing her body more firmly against his. "I figured if the shirt didn't work, full-on naked would do the trick."

"You do the trick all on your own," he murmured, lifting her up.

She clung tighter, smiling against his mouth as he maneuvered her onto the bed. He should resist. He knew he should resist, but she smiled up at him from beneath his body, and who had that kind of willpower? He'd wanted her since she'd reached for the gun in her desk all those days ago, and it had only intensified each second of getting to know her.

She was beautiful and seemed so sure, but he knew she'd been sheltered. She was untouched.

Except she wanted him, and she might be innocent, there might even be hidden fragile pieces of her, but Alyssa Jimenez knew what she wanted, and who was he to keep it from her?

"After all this is done, I can't promise—"

"I didn't ask you to promise anything, Ben."

He scowled. "Don't call me that."

Her mouth curved. "Why do you hate it so much?"

"It isn't my name."

"Hmm," she murmured, tracing his hairline with her index fingers. "It's half of your name. Why don't you like it?"

Bennet sighed. He had *no* idea why they were talking about this when they could be doing far more interesting things that she'd initiated, but he also knew she wouldn't just let it go. "It was my grandfather's name. Well, Bennet was, but he went by Ben. Everyone loved him."

"It doesn't sound like you did."

"He used to hit me."

Everything on Alyssa's face morphed into shocked outrage. "What do you mean hit you?"

"It's the Stevens way. Beat you into proper behavior."

"And your parents *agreed* with that?"

"They didn't practice it themselves, but they didn't stop it either. You can hardly be shocked by that. You grew up in a cartel. You must have seen far worse things."

"I was sheltered from the good and the bad, I suppose." She studied his face then wiggled beneath him. "Let's focus on the good right now, huh?"

"Yes, I like the sound of that. Why don't you unbutton the rest of that shirt?"

She smiled up at him as she brought her fingers to the buttons that were still buttoned. She pushed one button free, and then the next, and next until they were all free and he could pull the fabric apart and reveal her body completely.

She was petite, all bronze skin and slight curves. Everything inside him tensed and hardened.

"You're beautiful." And his, somehow. She was his.

ALYSSA DIDN'T QUITE know how to handle Bennet's words. Whether it was that sad little story about his grandfather, or telling her she was beautiful with such awe she almost believed it.

So, she pulled his head down and kissed him, because she knew what to do with her mouth then. Absorb the warmth of him, trace his lips with her tongue until he groaned and invaded her mouth with his.

She pressed her naked body to the rough fabric of his jeans and then pulled at the hem of his shirt, wanting to feel *him* against her. Skin and skin and hearts beating erratically against each other.

He pulled the shirt up and off his body, discarding it on the floor before his mouth returned to hers. But only briefly. Then it was moving down her jaw, her neck, feather-light brushes, the occasional brush of his tongue.

His palm slid up her stomach and rib cage until he was cupping her breast, kissing down her chest until his tongue touched her nipple. Her body would have jerked off the bed if Bennet hadn't been above her, a solid, warm wall of muscle.

She felt as though she was pulsing with something. Need probably, because the more his tongue played with her nipple the more restless she became—needing to move, needing to press against him, needing more. More, so much more.

But he seemed content to kiss and lick her everywhere but where she needed him most.

Nothing in the whole world had ever felt like this. Not the sight of the sun after two years of confinement. Not the closure on someone's face when she put a dangerous skip away. Nothing. Nothing had this kind of physical and emotional charge to it.

"Let me go get a condom," he said in a raspy voice that sizzled over her skin.

"You have condoms?" she asked dazedly.

"Sure. Rangers are like Boy Scouts. Always prepared."

"I hope Boy Scouts aren't prepared in *that* way," she called after him when he disappeared into the bathroom. When he reappeared, she grinned at him. "Wait. Please tell me you were a Boy Scout."

"Of course I was. Made it all the way up to Eagle Scout. You have no idea the things I can do with my hands." He grinned.

She spread out on his bed. "Show me."

He tossed the condom on the bed then undid his belt, eyes never leaving hers. Goose bumps rose on her skin at that steady, brazen gaze. He thought she was beautiful. He wanted her as much as she wanted him.

And still that need coiled deeper, no matter that she didn't think it could. She could barely sit still as he pushed his jeans and boxers off in one quick push, and then he was standing there naked.

He was just always so impressive. Tall and strong and broad. Long and hard and something close to intimidating. But no matter how nerves hammered in her chest, she didn't even think of backing out or changing her mind.

Not because she only wanted something good or to cross some adult rite of passage off the list, but because she wanted him. Only him.

He slid onto the bed, over her again, spreading

her legs apart with his knees. His fingers trailed up her calves, over her knees, her thighs.

She should do something, too, but all she could seem to do was lie there and breathe, watching his blue eyes intent on the most intimate part of her. He stroked her there and she whimpered, much to her own chagrin.

But his fingers *were* like magic. Sparking, spiraling the pleasure of magic as they entered and stroked, found places inside her that had her panting, writhing, pleading. She'd never felt this out of control, this desperate for something, except freedom.

But she didn't want freedom now. Not from Bennet. She wanted more of him. More of him inside her, on top of her.

"Please," she whispered, so close to some unknown cliff she didn't understand but knew she wanted to fall over. Over and over again.

He paused for a second, grabbing the condom and pulling it out of its package. She watched as he rolled the condom on his thick erection, and Alyssa couldn't quite fight the little kernel of panic that settled in her chest. "Bennet."

His blue eyes met hers, sure and steady as he positioned himself at her entrance. "Shh. It's all right. I'll take care of you."

She relaxed. "I know." It'd probably be easier if she could stop believing in people, but everyone who'd come into her life since she'd left that bunker had proved to her that her brothers' betrayal was their shortcoming. Not hers.

She could feel the tip of him slowly take the place of where his fingers had been. She was still pulsing with that lost orgasm, and as he slowly pushed inside she tried to chase that almost pleasure as much as she tried to ignore the uncomfortable tightness.

Everything was too big and too much, and yet everything she'd wanted was right there. Bennet inside her, Bennet on top of her, Bennet. Hers.

He moved, and there was a dull pain mixed in with that pleasure, but it was diluted enough she could enjoy that pleasure. Chase that joy that needed release. He moved slowly, his body hard against hers, and it made her feel safe. Protected.

All without being locked in or hidden away. He was bringing her to life even as he made sure nothing bad happened to her.

"Alyssa," he said, sounding pained, and that's when she realized a few tears had escaped her cheeks.

"It's not bad crying," she managed, because it wasn't. It was a release like any other. Too many emotions and feelings built up and leaking out.

"Good." He kissed a tear, his hand curling around her hip, angling himself differently, and this time when he slid deep, she gasped.

So, he did it again. And she forgot about that odd fullness and focused instead on the way he pulsed through her, uncoiled that heavy tight knot deep in her belly. This time she moved with him, and something seemed to explode inside her, waving through her, an intense, pulsing pleasure she wanted to bask in forever.

And still he moved inside her, making it all last longer, spiral harder, brighter. Until he was pushing deep, groaning and holding her tight to him.

She was so crushed to him she couldn't even wrap her arms around him like she wanted to. She wanted to hold on and never let go.

Someday you'll have to let go.

She closed her eyes against that thought, listening to the heavy beating of his heart. This was just like any other captivity. You only had the time you had. She'd enjoy it while she had it.

"Don't sleep on the window seat tonight," she said into his chest.

His mouth brushed across her temple. "I won't."

Chapter Thirteen

Bennet knew they were falling into too much of a routine, and yet he couldn't seem to help himself. What man in his right mind could?

They explored each other at night, researched all angles of the case during the day and sometimes distracted themselves with more sex then, too.

They hadn't gotten anywhere, and it should irk him more than it did. But it was hard to be irked about anything with Alyssa in his bed.

Even now, when they were both dressed, focused on reading through different things to do with Dom Cochrane's case. It felt…right. Right to be working in the company of someone he could quickly talk into getting naked.

Which seemed like a hell of an idea right now, since they'd have to start getting ready for the gala soon. He slid the laptop off his lap and rolled onto his side.

Alyssa was engrossed in the papers she'd been

rifling through, her eyebrows drawn together, her bottom lip pulled between her teeth.

The feeling in his chest scared him more than a little. He'd told her he couldn't make her any promises a few days ago, but every time he looked at her he wanted to make a million. He wanted to make sure she was always with him.

There was something warped in that probably, but no matter how often he told himself he was being an idiot, he wanted her beyond measure. In bed and out. Now and later. She just seemed to belong here, at his side.

So, he tugged one of the papers out of her hand, but she slapped his hand away. "Wait."

"My charm can't be wearing off *this* quickly."

"No, I think I've got something. Bennet, what if…" She arranged some papers he'd printed off for her. The picture of Salvador Dominguez and one of her brothers. The paperwork on Dom Cochrane's murder case.

She spread them all out, pointing at the pictures of Dom and Salvador. "What if Sal Cochrane, Dom Cochrane and Salvador Dominguez are all the same person, just different aliases? They've got the same nose. Same mouth. Salvador is older, obviously, but it has been sixteen years."

"Salvador has a clear scar on his chin."

"He could have gotten it in the time between pictures."

Bennet rubbed a hand against his jaw. "And if

that's true, a man who worked for your father got out of jail, started a new identity and built a cartel to rival your father's. And is now a donor to my mother's campaign."

Alyssa blew out a breath. "What reason would she have?"

"I don't know. Getting donations has never been a problem for the Stevenses, but perhaps things have gone south and I don't know about it."

"Maybe they're not the same person."

"He was convicted. Dom was convicted of murder, a murder that was probably ordered or sanctioned by your father. Yeah?"

Alyssa nodded, studying the pictures, so he did, too. Dom Cochrane and Salvador Dominguez certainly did look alike if you looked hard enough.

"Typically a cartel doesn't let that happen. They don't want one of their own talking to lawyers. They don't want to risk connections."

"I guess that's true, but he was the one stupid enough to get caught."

When he raised an eyebrow at her, she shrugged. "That's how they'd think about it. He got caught, and we never have. I love my brothers, Bennet, because… Well, a lot of complicated reasons, but I'm under no illusion they're good men or have never killed anyone. It's the life."

"Why were you sheltered from it?"

"I'm a girl." She shrugged again. "It's the only reason I ever got. Even before my mother left or whatever it is that happened, the way they'd talk about her... They thought she was weak, and maybe she was. She never spent much time with me."

"So, what was she doing if she wasn't spending time with her daughter and was too weak to be part of things?"

"I don't know."

Bennet studied the pictures again. "Let's work off the theory they're all the same man. Dom Cochrane had orders from your father to kill someone as part of cartel business. Dom gets caught, tried, sent to prison. Who would Dom be most angry with?"

"My father, but like I said, my father hasn't been well for years. Years upon years. CJ runs the show."

"So, maybe he transfers the revenge. It's personal enough, and the cartel family is actual family. It all works together."

"Except one of my brothers meeting with him."

"You still don't know which one?"

"It would make the most sense if it was CJ. He's the head of things, and it would make sense if Dad passed that earring on to him, but... It doesn't look like CJ to me. Something about the hand."

"What about it?"

"CJ is always angry. Fists clenched or on a weapon. My other brothers are always armed, except Oscar." She paused, her finger touching the hand of the man in the picture. "It can't be Oscar," she whispered, shaking her head. "But everything points to Oscar."

"Are you certain?"

"No. But he taps his fingers on his legs when he's nervous. Did you see him do it at my office? He's always done it. This man's fingers are on his leg, as if he's tapping them out of sight of Dominguez."

She looked up at him, her expression sad and a little lost. "Oscar was the sweet one, sweet to me. I can't believe he'd double-cross the family. It's not in him. Not like the others."

"So, maybe it's not him."

Alyssa swallowed and nodded, looking back at the picture of Dominguez. "How did we turn out okay? I mean, assuming your parents are part of this. How did we…"

"You know, I learned something from dear old Grandpa Ben."

She frowned and reached out and touched his cheek. "I don't like your making light of that."

"You can't beat who someone is out of them or beat who you are into them. I'm not saying it doesn't shape them or leave a mark, but it never does exactly what the bad wants it to do." He took her hand and kissed her palm. "We are who we are because that's what we are."

"So, we'll still be what we are after this is all over?"

Which wasn't as simple a question as he'd like. She was the daughter of a drug cartel kingpin, and whether his mother was involved in all this or not, he was the son of a US senator and, more, he was a Texas Ranger. It would be complicated. It would be…

She withdrew her hand from his, and he wished he had the words to make it right. To say they could be.

"Your hair lady is going to be here soon."

"My nothing. *Your* hair lady. *Your* dress. *Your* party."

"I'll pass on wearing a dress tonight, but we need to go over the plan one more time," he said, ignoring her irritation, really ignoring her hurt. They didn't have time for that. Not right this second. Afterward when he could work it all out, he'd figure them out, too, but they had to do this first.

Alyssa rolled her eyes. "Never leave each other's side. Be on the lookout for Dominguez and anyone he talks to. File as much away as we can, and if we have the opportunity to follow him we do, as long as we're together. That about cover it?"

"Trust no one."

"Except you."

"We'll trust each other."

A knock sounded at the door, and Alyssa sighed heavily.

"Who is it?" Bennet called.

"Ms. Delaney is here," Kinsey returned.

Bennet got off the bed and headed for the door to let Tawny in.

"Wait. Tawny's doing my hair and makeup?"

"When I asked her for referrals for someone, she suggested herself. I figured that'd work out, keep fewer new people from traipsing in and out."

"If I look ridiculous after this, I'm blaming you," Alyssa muttered.

"Be very hard on me. I probably deserve it," he replied, grinning at her as he opened the door.

ALYSSA FELT LIKE HYPERVENTILATING. Tawny had done her hair and makeup, chattering on and on about statement colors, and had put diamonds around her neck, and all Alyssa could think was this was all wrong.

Tawny should be going to this party, talking to debutantes and rich politicians and whatever. Alyssa should be in a little apartment above her friends' garage in her jeans and T-shirt, considering her next bounty-hunting case.

But Alyssa was in some expensive gown, her hair swept back in ways she never would have dreamed it could be curled and coiffed. She was wearing lipstick of all things, and anytime she caught a glimpse of herself in the mirror, she wanted to rip off the weird little gold hairpiece Tawny had pinned into her hair and run screaming in the opposite direction.

But Bennet was counting on her, and no matter how he'd hesitated when she'd mentioned *after* earlier, she couldn't let him down. He'd given her too much, even if they were coming to the end of that particular line.

"Now, I know you don't want to draw too much attention, but I brought two possible pairs of shoes. One is the sensible choice, and one is the little flash-of-fun choice." Tawny pulled out two pairs of heels from her bag.

Heels. Tall, tall, impossible-looking heels.

"I've never walked in heels before."

"Never walked in… Honey, where *did* you come from?"

Now that was a question.

"They aren't any different from regular shoes. Mostly," Tawny offered brightly.

"I don't believe that for a second."

Tawny laughed. "Okay, it requires some balance and some…well, beauty is pain and whatnot." She handed Alyssa the less flashy pair. "Here, these are shorter."

Alyssa slid her feet into the heels and tried not to wince as she stood.

"Just balance on your heels and it'll be all good. Besides, Ben will catch you if you fall."

"Did he ever tell you why he doesn't like that?" Alyssa asked, failing at the breezy, conversational tone Tawny always used.

"Like what?"

"Shortening his name to Ben."

Tawny cocked her head. "No. Why?"

Alyssa knew she shouldn't say anything. It was none of her business. But, well, Bennet was always protecting *her*. Maybe it was time for her to do the same for him. "Maybe you just shouldn't."

Tawny stood there and didn't say anything for the longest time. Eventually, she nodded. "All right.

Well, you're all finished. I'll leave you to make a grand entrance." Tawny collected all her things and opened the door with a wink.

"Hey, um, I know you're getting paid for this and all, but thanks. I appreciate it."

Tawny smiled that big, pretty smile Alyssa knew even with years of practice she wouldn't be able to duplicate. "You're very welcome, Alyssa. Good luck to you." She slid outside, and Alyssa knew she had to follow. No matter how desperately she wanted to avoid *any* gala, but especially *this* gala, it was a job. One she had to do well.

Which meant she had to ditch the heels. She kicked them off and grabbed her tennis shoes. The dress was long enough it would cover the faux pas, she hoped. And if not, well, hell, she'd at least have the ability to run if she needed to, and the dress was already enough of a detriment.

A knock sounded on the bathroom door. "Are you coming?" Bennet demanded. "Tawny said you were done."

Alyssa took a deep breath and took a few halting steps toward the door. All the nerves were just worry over what they might find out tonight and what danger they might be in. It had nothing to do with Bennet seeing her in this getup.

"Don't say anything stupid," she called through the door.

"Well, thank you for that wonderful vote of confidence. Now, would you get the hell out here so we can—" He stopped abruptly as she stepped into the bedroom.

Then he didn't say anything at all. He didn't even move. He just stared at her. Expressionless.

Alyssa fidgeted. "I know I said don't say anything stupid, but you could say *something*."

"You…" He reached out and touched the cascade of golden circle things Tawny had fastened into her upswept hair. "You look like some kind of goddess."

"That counts as stupid."

"That counts as a compliment," he returned, leaning in.

She shoved him back. "You cannot ruin my makeup. I don't know how to fix it. Besides, you said we needed to get going."

"I think I changed my mind." His hands landed on her hips, and no matter how she pushed him away, his mouth brushed her neck.

And, okay, maybe she didn't push all that hard. It was entirely possible she just sighed and leaned into him while his mouth did unfathomable things to her neck.

She didn't want to go out there. She didn't want to face strangers or even try to solve a mystery or catch any bad guys. She wanted to stay right here, because once they did all that solving and catching, she wasn't so sure right here would exist anymore.

Since that caused an annoying lump in her throat, she gave him a little nudge. "We have to go."

He sighed heavily against her neck, but he pulled

away. He looked her in the eye, Mr. Texas Ranger all over his face.

"We're going to go over this one more time—"

"Bennet."

"We don't separate unless absolutely necessary. You have your cell phone, your knife and your gun on you at all times." He swept his gaze over her. "Where the hell did you put the gun?"

She grinned, lifting the long skirt up to her hip, where a thigh holster held her Glock. "I mean, God help me if I need it quickly, but at least it's there."

"And the knife is in your bra?"

"Always."

He grinned. "A very, very unique goddess." He cocked his head as his gaze followed her dress hem back down to the floor. "Are you wearing tennis shoes?"

"Don't you dare tell Tawny. She'll kill me."

Bennet chuckled as they moved toward the door, but any humor left them both. What lay ahead of them was risky, and potentially dangerous, most especially for her since her attacker a few days ago had said she'd be dead within the week.

But that only made her more determined. She'd been through one horrible thing in her life already with the kidnapping, and no pissant minion who botched the simplest kidnapping attempt was going to make her cower in fear.

Dead within the week? Not without a fight.

Bennet stopped abruptly with his hand on the

knob. He turned to face her, staring at her intently, and Alyssa didn't know what he was looking for, what there was to say in this moment.

"No unnecessary risks," he said eventually.

"What if it leads to the answer?"

He released the knob and curled his fingers around her upper arm. Hard. "No unnecessary risks. Promise me." No jokes, no charming smiles. This wasn't even that Texas Ranger stoicism thing he had down so well. It was dark and dangerous.

But she wasn't about to promise things he wouldn't. "You first."

His mouth flattened into a grim line, and the tight grip he had on her arm didn't loosen.

"No unnecessary risks is a two-way street, Bennet. Either we both take them, or neither of us do."

It took him another few seconds of whatever inner arguing he was doing to speak. "Fine. Neither."

Which was not the answer she had expected in the least. "But… We have to figure this out. It's your important case. It's my mother's murder. You can't honestly think we should play it safe."

"Yes, that's what I honestly think," he replied grimly.

"Why? When we've worked so—"

He took her other arm, giving her a little shake. "You mean more to me than whatever this is," he said, so darkly, so seriously, Alyssa could hardly catch her breath.

He blinked, his grip loosening, as if he was a little surprised at his own vehemence. "So, we play it safe. Got it?"

She could only stare at him. Mean more to him? When had she ever meant more to someone? When had her safety ever been paramount to an end result? Oh, her brothers had kept her safe for twenty years, but for the cartel. She'd been a burden and a duty, not something someone cared about. She'd maybe never thought of it that way, but she understood it now.

Understood it because she'd never felt like a burden to Bennet. She felt…important. Central.

"Alyssa."

She nodded stupidly. "I got it." She swallowed down all the tremulous emotion in her throat. "No risks."

He released her from his grip, holding out his elbow with one arm and opening the door with his other hand. "Then, let's go."

She slipped her arm through his, still looking up at the hard planes of his face. Clean-shaven and so dashing-looking in his suit. And she meant something to him. Something enough that he'd rather her be safe than solve this case that had been so important to him just days ago.

It was a big deal, no matter what she tried to tell herself. It was a big deal he'd think that, say that, prioritize keeping her safe over solving this case.

He led her to the staircase, and she had to focus on the steps instead of his handsome face. Even though everyone in the house would be attending the party, it was still decorated to the hilt. Christmas lights and evergreen garlands sparkled over the curving banister of the grand staircase.

The floor gleamed, clean and expensive. Even the wood trim seemed to glow in the twinkle of the Christmas lights. The Christmas tree shone bright white from the living room, and it was like walking through a magazine or a castle or anything but anywhere she belonged.

She'd never fit into this sparkling world of wealth and appearances. No matter how many dresses Bennet bought for her or how often Tawny did her makeup. She was a Jimenez. Criminal by association no matter whom she might help bring down.

Bennet could never accept that. She might mean something to him, but once this case was over, the only way they could go was in opposite directions.

So, there was no use getting her hopes up and, more, no use keeping her promise.

Chapter Fourteen

Bennet scanned the crowd for a flash of anyone who might resemble the photograph he had of Salvador Dominguez. He scanned the crowd for any of Alyssa's brothers. He scanned the crowd over and over again.

But all he ever saw were legions of his parents' friends and donors and Texas elite. From the looks of it, Alyssa was just as frustrated about it as he was.

"Let's dance."

Alyssa grimaced. "You think I know how to dance?"

"It's just swaying to a beat." He used the arm that had been situated around her waist the whole evening to lead her to the small cluster of people dancing to slow, jazzy Christmas music. Once on a corner of the dance floor under sparkling lights and all the sparkling jewels on bodies all around them, he drew her close.

She put one hand on his arm and the other she clearly had no idea what to do with. He took it in his, placing it on his shoulder. He eased her into a simple side-to-side step.

"Why do you know how to dance?" she grumbled. "They teach that at Texas Ranger school?"

"Cotillion."

She wrinkled her nose. "What the hell is that?"

He laughed, drawing her even closer. "If I explained it, it would only horrify you."

"That I believe." Her gaze did another scan of the room before returning to his. "Is he not coming? Is he hiding?" she whispered.

"I don't know."

"This is crazy-making, all these questions. All this waiting. Why doesn't he grow a pair and make a move?"

Bennet wanted to laugh, but the thought of any one of the numerous potential "bad guys" out there making a move filled him with dread. They'd already been too close to Alyssa being hurt.

But all he could do was sway to the music, holding her close and watching the room diligently. Maybe whoever it was—Sal or Dom Cochrane, Salvador Dominguez or one of Alyssa's brothers—wouldn't dare try anything as long as he was by her side.

Well, if that were the case, he wouldn't leave it. And no matter how much she'd chafe at the idea, it didn't bother him in the least.

A moody version of "I'll Be Home for Christmas" started playing, and Alyssa rested her cheek against his chest, and he could all but feel the sadness waving off her.

He wanted to promise he'd get her back to her old life by Christmas next week, but how could he possibly promise that? No matter how many little clues they managed to put together, they were still as in the dark about the end game as they'd ever been.

"It'll be all right," he murmured, rubbing a hand down her back and up again.

She sniffled a little. "What if they don't forgive me?"

"Who?"

"Gabby and Natalie. I haven't visited the baby. I've been ignoring their calls. If I miss Christmas… What if they don't forgive me? It's not like we're related by blood or anything. They don't owe me anything, and then I'd be alone. Again."

"You won't be alone." No matter how many qualms he had about what might happen *after*, he couldn't imagine his life anymore without Alyssa in it. Didn't want to.

She'd stiffened in his arms, and she didn't raise her head. He could all but feel the questions in her, but she didn't voice any of them.

"Besides, they'll forgive you. Even if you're not blood related, they're family, and you'll be able to explain this all to them afterward. They'll understand. They know how these kinds of things work. Not only are they both involved with law enforcement, but they've both been in danger before. They know what it's like."

She finally pulled her head back and looked up at him. "Did you really mean—"

There was a tap on Bennet's shoulder and a loud, booming voice. "May I cut in?"

Bennet glanced back at his father, who had his best politician's smile plastered on his face. Bennet tried to fight the scowl that wanted to take over his mouth.

"You've been hiding your date all night, Bennet," Dad said jovially, clapping him on the back a little hard. "Let one of us old hats have a turn."

"It looks like your mother's free," Alyssa said, nodding toward Mom walking away from the cluster she'd been talking with earlier. "Why don't you go dance with her?"

He should. He should do some digging about Sal Cochrane here where things would be so busy and booze-filled Mom was likely to forget his questioning in the morning. And Alyssa wasn't just a grown woman, but a capable, *armed* grown woman who could handle his father for a quick dance. Even if Dad said something asinine.

He wanted to finish their conversation. He wanted to assure her he meant *everything*. And he downright hated the thought of leaving her, stupid as it was.

But what could happen to her if she was dancing with Dad? It wasn't like whoever they were waiting for was going to pop out and snatch her away when she was dancing with a US senator, for God's sake.

"All right," Bennet said, smiling tightly and probably not at all convincingly. "Just return her to me after the song, huh?"

Dad rolled his eyes, taking Alyssa's hand off Bennet's shoulder and clutching it in his own.

"Such a caveman I raised, Alyssa. I hope this boy has a few more manners than that." Dad slid his arm around Alyssa's waist and started leading her away.

Bennet stood at the corner of the dance floor like a fool. Dad was either trying to piss him off or... Well, no, probably just trying to irritate him. Bennet shouldn't let him win.

He forced himself to walk over to his mother, tried to make the scowl on his face soften into something bordering on pleasant.

"Are you having fun?" Mom asked.

"The time of my life," Bennet replied drily, causing his mother to chuckle.

"You look quite cozy with that girl."

Bennet merely grunted. Once the case was figured out he'd fight Mom on this battle, but not before. For now, he'd be as discreet and noncommittal as possible.

"You know, there were a few names on the guest list I didn't recognize," he offered, failing hard at casual.

"Worried about security, dear?"

"Something like that. I don't remember you ever mentioning Sal Cochrane before."

Mother's eyebrows drew together. "Cochrane. That name doesn't ring any bells."

"He's a donor of yours."

Mom chuckled. "No. Honey, trust me. I know all my donors. I make sure of it."

Bennet frowned. Mom could be lying, he supposed, but he knew his mother fairly well. He knew her politician charm and the way lies could fall out of her mouth with the utmost authenticity, but she was rarely flippant about lying.

He pulled out his phone and brought up the email from Dad's assistant with the donor list and handed it to her. "It says Sal Cochrane right here."

Mom took the phone and squinted at the screen before scrolling. "Mariah must have made some kind of mistake. This isn't my donor list."

"You're certain?"

Mom nodded, scrolling more "Julie Dyer is on it. Trust me, she wouldn't give me a cent if her life depended on it. That's your father's donor list." She handed the phone back to him, and Bennet nearly dropped it.

If this was Dad's list, then Dad was the connection.

And he was dancing with Alyssa.

THE WHOLE NOT-KNOWING-HOW-TO-DANCE thing was a little less concerning when she was dancing with Bennet. Dancing with his father, no matter that there was far more distance between their bodies, made her inordinately tense.

"This is a nice…party. Gala. Thing." Alyssa wanted the floor to swallow her whole. She sounded like an idiot.

"My wife just loves her…party gala things," Mr. Stevens replied with a wink.

Alyssa took a deep breath and tried to relax. Mr. Stevens was nice. A little slick, but nice nonetheless. None of Mrs. Stevens's ice.

"Are you all right, dear? You're looking a little peaked. Why don't we step out onto the balcony? Get a little fresh air."

"No, I'm all right."

But Mr. Stevens was tugging her through the swaying throng of dance-floor people and across the room.

Alyssa wasn't quite sure what was going on, but something didn't sit right. She glanced over at where Bennet had been. His head was bent over his phone as he talked to his mother.

Mr. Stevens all but pulled her onto the balcony, and she was about to scream, jerk her hand away, anything, but there were people on the balcony, even a waiter carrying around trays of champagne with little red fruit floating in the top, sprigs of what looked like holly decorating the bottom of the glass.

It could hardly be that sinister if there were plenty of people around. It could hardly be that sinister considering Mr. Stevens looked downright jolly.

Mr. Stevens took two champagne flutes as a waiter passed, handing her one. She took it even though she had no plans to drink it.

"Now, you've made quite an impression on my son, and that is a hard thing to do. God knows he'll keep you away from my wife and me as long as that's the case, so I wanted to corner you a bit. I hope you don't mind."

"Well, um, no. I guess not," she managed. It was stupid to want to impress him, please him, but no matter how strained Bennet's relationship might be with his parents, he did love them. And no matter how she told herself there was no future for her and Bennet... She couldn't quite bring herself to blow up that tiniest inkling of a chance.

"Tell me about yourself, Alyssa." He took a sip of his champagne, looking like some ritzy watch or cologne ad.

"Oh, well, there's not a whole lot to tell."

"Where'd you grow up? What do you do? How'd you meet my son?"

Alyssa opened her mouth, hoping some kind of lie would just fall out, but it didn't. Nothing did. Not even a squeak.

"Are they really that difficult of questions, Ms. Jimenez?"

Alyssa froze. He knew her name, and something about that slick smile that had never quite settled right with her now suddenly seemed sinister.

But he was as relaxed as ever, watching her as he sipped champagne and waited for her to answer.

"Cat got your tongue? Have a few drinks. Might loosen things up for you."

Alyssa swallowed, trying to think straight and not panic. "What exactly is it that you want from me?"

"I'm just concerned about my son, Alyssa. Surely you understand what kind of good, upstanding man Bennet is. He has such a clear sense of right and wrong. I'd hate for him to get wrapped up in the wrong kind of people and get himself hurt."

"Your son can take care of himself," she returned, trying to figure out an exit strategy that wouldn't draw attention. But the people on the balcony were dwindling, and the waiter had disappeared.

Pretty soon she'd be out here alone with Mr. Stevens, and she didn't think that would be very good at all.

"Are you so sure about that?" He said it so casually, so offhandedly, it shouldn't mean anything. It couldn't mean anything, but Alyssa couldn't help but read it as a threat.

This was all wrong. All wrong.

"I should get back," she muttered, taking a retreating step backward.

Mr. Stevens's hand shot out and clamped onto her wrist in less than the blink of an eye. "Now, now, Ms. Jimenez. Surely you don't need to rush off just yet."

"Let go of me," Alyssa said between gritted teeth.

She tugged at her arm, but he held fast, something in his expression hardening.

Alyssa wanted to panic, but she fought it off. She just had to break his grasp and run inside and to Bennet. She could always grab one of her weapons with her free hand, but she didn't think waving a knife or gun at a US senator for some veiled threats was going to go over very well.

She heard the click of a door and jumped, jerking her gaze to the doors that led to the balcony. The now-empty balcony, one door shut and, if that clicking sound was any indication, locked.

But there was still one open. She just had to break his grasp and get through it.

She pulled hard, but Mr. Stevens only jerked her toward him.

"What is this?" she demanded.

"This, Ms. Jimenez, is business. Now, I suggest you stop trying to put up a fight. I'd hate to bruise that pretty face of yours, and I'd hate to have to get my son involved. Bennet's an excellent policeman, but we both know he'd put himself in harm's way before he let you be put in it."

"You would hurt your own son?" she asked incredulously.

"Oh, Ms. Jimenez, I'll do whatever I have to."

Before he finished the sentence, Alyssa pivoted and elbowed Mr. Stevens as hard as she could in the chest. He stumbled back, releasing her grasp, and she ran for the open door.

But a man stepped through, closing it behind him. Alyssa stopped short at the sight of her youngest brother blocking her exit.

"Oscar, what are you doing?" She took a few more steps toward him, reaching out to him. Even if Oscar was working with Mr. Stevens, he wouldn't hurt her. "Oscar, you have to help me," she whispered, looking at him imploringly. "Let me through. Please."

"Sorry, Lyss," Oscar said, sounding truly regretful.

Before she could beg, or push him out of the way, pain exploded in her head. And then there was nothing but darkness.

Chapter Fifteen

"You're sure he came this way?" Bennet demanded of the shaking waiter who was leading him down a back hallway out of the hotel.

"Y-yes, sir."

"Then where the hell is he?" Dad and Alyssa hadn't been anywhere in the ballroom. No hallways, no bathrooms. Bennet had tactlessly started asking questions, all the glitzy attendees of the ball looking like he was crazy, but the waiter had spoken up and said he'd seen Dad.

But there was no sign of him or Alyssa. There was nothing but an empty stretch of hallway. Bennet felt sick to his stomach. He didn't want to believe this of his father, but they'd been there one second, and gone the next.

Gone. Just gone. In the few minutes he'd discussed donors with his mother, they were suddenly nowhere to be found.

He scrubbed his hands over his face and focused on the waiter. "And you didn't see the woman either?"

"No. No woman. Nobody really. I mean. Except Mr. Stevens. Who went this way." The waiter swallowed with a loud gulp.

Something about the way the kid looked away and took in an unsteady breath poked at Bennet. He took a threatening step toward the shaking, sweating waiter. "Are you lying to me?" he demanded, getting in the guy's face.

"N-no, sir. Mr. Stevens… He told me… I mean…"

Bennet grasped the man's shirt in his fist and gave him a hard shake. "You are talking to a Texas Ranger in the middle of a life-or-death investigation, so if you want to keep your nose intact and your ass out of jail, you better start telling the truth."

The waiter started crying.

"Look, I don't know what he threatened you with, if anything, but if someone dies because you kept it to yourself, you're an accessory, and I will do everything in my power to punish you to the fullest extent of the law."

The waiter started crying even harder. "I don't know, man. I was just following orders. All he told me was to tell you he went this way, but I don't know where he went."

Bennet swore. A distraction. "What else do you know?" he demanded, giving the guy another hard shake.

"I don't know. I don't know," the man sobbed. "There was someone with him. A guy named Oscar. But that's all I know."

Bennet released the man and swore, barely acknowledging the waiter crumpling to the floor. He had to calm down and think. *Think.* What the hell could his father possibly be doing?

Oscar. Alyssa was so sure her youngest brother was the nice one, but Bennet couldn't let that console him right now. There were too many variables, and since he knew Alyssa would under no circumstances disappear of her own volition, they were all really shitty variables.

He didn't even know where to start. He had no idea what he was dealing with. All he knew was she was gone, and she wouldn't have done that to him.

Which meant he had to focus. He had to be the Texas Ranger he'd been trained to be. He had to find Mom. Based on the conversation he'd had with her earlier, he didn't think she was involved, but she would know all the places Dad could go.

He left the waiter sobbing on the floor and strode back toward the ballroom, but before he made it down the length of the back hallway, Mom pushed through some doors.

"Bennet. There you are. You've made something of a scene. What's going on?"

"I'll tell you what's going on. Your husband has kidnapped my…" What the hell was she? He didn't know. "I need a list of all the property you and Dad own jointly or separately. Emailed to my work address ASAP." He pushed past her. He'd start at the main house. It was a long shot, but maybe there'd be some clue in Dad's office or…

"Bennet, you don't honestly think—"

"You're right. I don't think, I know. I know what he did, what he's done." He turned to face her. "Mom, if you really have nothing to do with any of this, I'd suggest getting your lawyers together."

"What on earth are you even talking about? Bennet? Bennet! I don't have any earthly clue—"

"My, my. What is all this commotion?"

Bennet turned incredulously to find his father pushing through the doors, then standing there, brushing at his sleeve as if there was some minuscule piece of lint. Pristine and politician perfect in his suit as if everything was fine. Normal.

Bennet lunged, missing only because two of Dad's plainclothes security guards stepped in and grabbed him, holding him back. "Where is she?" he demanded, shoving against the guards.

Dad had the gall to look incredulous and quizzical. "Where is who?"

"You were the last one with her. Now I want to know what you've done with her."

"You mean Alyssa? Oh, she said something about going to the bathroom and—"

"Bullshit," Bennet spat. "You don't think I've put it all together? You and Dominguez and Jimenez. I've got more evidence than you can possibly imagine, and if you think kidnapping her—"

"You aren't making any sense, son. Should I perhaps put in a call to Captain Dean? I have to say I have been worried about your mental state as of late."

Bennet laughed. As if the threat of his job would get through this haze of fury and fear. "Come after me, Dad. Throw it all at me. I will destroy you," Bennet said and then, with a well-placed elbow, escaped the security guard's pathetic hold and pushed past his father and back into the ballroom.

It was teeming with people, many who gave him odd looks, and there was just too much of a world out there. He couldn't do this on his own.

He hadn't wanted to bring in anyone else this whole time because it was his case to solve, but Alyssa's safety trumped all of it. He would find her, and if anyone had hurt her he'd kill them himself.

He pulled his phone out of his pocket, jogging through the ballroom to the exit to the parking lot. He searched his email for an old correspondence with Jaime Alessandro over The Stallion case, found the phone number he needed and called.

"Hello?" Alessandro answered, clearly skeptical at the unknown number.

"Agent Alessandro, this is Bennet Stevens with the Texas Rangers."

"Ah, yes, I've been hearing your name quite a bit around these parts. Not exactly kindly."

Which might have been funny in any other situation. "I need your help. Alyssa needs your help."

There wasn't a second of hesitation. "I'm all ears."

WHEN ALYSSA CAME TO, head throbbing painfully, stomach roiling, she was in a basement of some kind. She took a deep breath in and out to fight the nausea and the panic at the realization she was tied to a chair, her hands behind her back, her ankles each to a leg of the chair, and then another cord around her thighs and the seat of the chair.

But she could see, and she could breathe. Important things to focus on. If she panicked, nothing good could happen. If she panicked, she *would* end up dead.

Of course, how she was still alive was a mystery. Surely a US senator wasn't going to leave loose ends lying around. *If* she escaped his life would be over.

And what will Bennet think of that?

She had to close her eyes against the painful thought of Bennet. He would not be taking any of this well. But he would save her. He would. He knew the last person she'd been with was his father.

And he's going to choose saving you over bringing his father down?

She couldn't think like that. Besides, Mr. Stevens had said it himself. Bennet had a clear sense of right and wrong. Even if he wanted to protect his father, his conscience wouldn't allow him to do it at her expense.

She hoped.

She was still in her dress, but she could tell the gun she'd had strapped to her thigh was gone. She could feel the outline of her knife against her breast, and that was good. If she could get untied, she had a chance.

Something sounded behind her, a squeak and groan. A door opening maybe. She tried to turn her head, but the way her arms were tied behind her back limited how much she could look back.

Footsteps approached, and Alyssa did everything in her power to breathe normally. To stay focused and calm no matter who appeared.

"You're awake. Good," Oscar offered cheerfully.

Alyssa could only stare at her brother as he stepped in front of her. He'd knocked her out, and by all accounts was the one who'd tied her up here, and he was acting as if it was all normal.

"You hit me."

"You didn't listen," he returned as if they were arguing semantics, not whether or not he'd knocked her out in the middle of a party.

"What is going on?" she said, her breathing coming too fast, the panic rising too hard. "Oscar, please, explain this to me." She might have tried to hold back the tears, but she had to hope they would get through to her brother. Her sweet brother. How could he be doing this to her?

"You should have listened to me, Lyss." Oscar paced the concrete room, tapping his fingers on his leg. "I'm running out of options here. Why'd you have to keep pushing? I could have kept you out of this if you'd only listened."

"Kept me out of *what*?"

"He wants you."

"Who? Stevens?"

Oscar laughed. "Please. Gary Stevens is nothing more than a pawn. A distraction to get you here. Dominguez is who you should be afraid of. He wants revenge, and it has to be you. Stevens only helped because Dominguez owns him."

"And Dominguez owns you?"

Again Oscar laughed. "No one owns me, Lyss. Dominguez and I are like partners."

"Why are you working for Dominguez?"

Oscar scoffed. "You have to ask that question? CJ wouldn't even let me carry a gun, or run a raid by myself. He thought I was stupid and weak. Well, he'll see who's stupid and weak now."

"Oscar. He's our brother. I'm your sister. Whatever is going on—"

"He killed our mother, you know. CJ. Our own brother. He killed her. And then he gave you over to The Stallion, all so The Stallion wouldn't encroach on cartel business."

Even though it confirmed too many suspicions, Alyssa could only shake her head, the tears falling faster now. "No."

"He did, Alyssa. On Dad's order he killed our mother. And when The Stallion threatened us and all we built, he offered you."

She couldn't get a full breath. She couldn't…

"Dominguez might not be blood, but he's honorable. He'd never ask me to kill you."

"But he had you kidnap me."

Oscar shrugged, as if that was neither here nor there.

"I'll die anyway. His men who tried to kidnap me last week said he wants me dead."

"But I won't be the one to do it. He'd never ask that of me."

Alyssa had no rebuttal for that. None at all. He didn't care if she died, as long as he didn't have to do it.

"He might not kill you, Lyss. If you can prove some worth, he might just keep you."

"Prove some… Have you lost your mind? Have you lost your heart? What happened to you?" Alyssa demanded, trying so very hard not to sob.

Oscar refused to meet her gaze, and the sound from before echoed in the concrete room. A door opening. Oscar straightened as footsteps approached.

"Good work, Oscar. I knew I could count on you," a booming voice said.

Oscar beamed and Alyssa thought she was going to throw up as a new man stepped into view. Definitely the man from the picture they had of Salvador Dominguez. Tall and lanky, his graying black hair pulled back in a ponytail, the faint scar on his chin. His dark eyes glittered with something that looked eerily close to joy.

"And here she is." He shook his head as if she was

some long-lost friend he was so happy to see. "You look just like your mother." He reached out to touch her cheek and Alyssa flinched, trying to back away from the touch but held too still by the ropes.

"Well, where are my manners? Introductions are necessary, of course. Salvador Dominguez, at your service." He made a strange little bow. "I know we haven't met yet, but I know so many of your family. Oscar here, of course. And I used to work for your father before he became something of an imbecile."

He smiled widely, and Alyssa tried to keep herself still, to not react at all.

Salvador cocked his head. "You don't seem surprised by that information. My, my, maybe you and your Ranger were more thorough than I gave you credit for. Good thing we moved when we did, Oscar." Salvador clapped Oscar on the back as he continued to smile at Alyssa. "Your brother is quite the prodigy. I've been very impressed."

Alyssa wished she could wipe the tears off her cheeks and put on some unemotional, screw-you manner. As it was, she couldn't imagine how foolish she looked tearstained, makeup streaked, hair falling out of all Tawny's ruthless pinning.

"A quiet one. How unlike the Jimenez clan. Even your mother was quite the chatterbox. Of course, I loved to listen to her chatter. You see, I loved her. What a beauty she was, and so…passionate." He reached out and touched her face again, the skim of his index finger down her cheek causing her to shudder as her stomach roiled more viciously.

Salvador leaned in close, so close she could feel his heavy breath on her neck. "I bet your Texas Ranger would say the same about you."

Alyssa wished she could throw up on him, but no matter how nauseated she felt, all she could do was sit there and try not to cry no matter how disgusting his breath felt across her bare skin.

"Don't worry, little girl, I would never test out that theory…in front of your brother," he whispered.

Alyssa worked on her best withering glare. "I don't know what you want, but—"

"Oh, that's simple," he said downright jovially, stepping back and straightening to his full height. "Your family let me rot in jail for years, and while I did, they killed the woman I loved." He waved his arms dramatically as he spoke. "So now, I'm going to kill you."

Alyssa didn't gasp. She didn't allow herself to. She simply stared at her brother imploringly, no matter how he avoided her gaze, until Salvador stepped between them.

"Eyes up here, beautiful."

"You won't kill me," she said, even if she wasn't certain she believed it. She wasn't going down without a fight. Without some backbone.

"Well, maybe not *now*. We might need to have a few *conversations* first, but then you will definitely die. On camera. For all of the Jimenezes to see."

Chapter Sixteen

Bennet and Jaime had split up the list of properties Mom had emailed him and were checking them out one by one. Austin PD was currently questioning his father and had put out an APB for Alyssa. To Bennet's surprise, Mom had snapped into her own kind of action, scouring Dad's financial records for any transactions that might give them a hint.

But still nothing was *happening*, and even as Bennet searched another of his father's Austin properties, he knew it was damn pointless. He was fighting a losing battle, and he didn't know what else to do.

His phone chimed, and he brought it to his ear. "Stevens."

"Gabby found something," Jaime said with no preamble.

"Gabby?"

"I figure if you can do a few things off the record, so can I. She's a better analyst than half my men anyway," Jaime muttered. "I had her look through the files on a raid the FBI did on a house a few months ago. We'd gathered information Salvador Dominguez was doing business there, but the raid found absolutely nothing."

"Well, that doesn't exactly sound promising," Bennet replied, heading back to his car after another property was completely empty.

"It doesn't. Until we tracked down the owner of the house. Originally we hit nothing but dead ends and fake LLCs, but Gabby discovered a tie to your father."

"Address," Bennet barked, starting his car.

"Austin, luckily. I'll text it to you and meet you there."

Bennet hit End and backed out of the parking lot and added the texted address into his GPS. It was all the way on the other side of the city, but the link to both Dominguez and his father was too much to ignore.

He flew through town, then slowed down as he approached the address, looking for an inconspicuous place to park his vehicle.

It was a nondescript-looking house in the middle of a very middle-class neighborhood. Dark had descended, but most of the houses in the neighborhood had lights of some kind on. Except this one. Dark shrouded it so much Bennet could barely make out anything, especially with a privacy fence extending around the front yard as well as the back. Bennet parked his car three houses down and got out of the car, trying to canvas the best way to approach.

If Alyssa was here, there had to be some kind of security in place. Not just alarms, but cameras surely, and if there'd been an FBI raid here a few months ago that had found nothing, surely they were not dealing with amateurs.

He wouldn't let that make him feel sick, because the most important thing wasn't anything except getting Alyssa out, and he'd do whatever it took. Whatever it took, enough that he had to pray she was here, and safe.

He glanced down the road as another car approached. It stopped five doors down and on the opposite side of the street. The headlights stayed on as Jaime got out casually, scanning the neighborhood in the exact way Bennet had. He nodded to Bennet and turned off the lights of his car, shrouding him back in darkness.

What had Bennet's hand resting on the butt of his weapon was another car three houses up from the current house parking as conspicuously. Of course, the minute the driver stepped out of the car and into the light of the streetlamp, Bennet could only stare.

"Is that Vaughn?" Jaime asked as he came up to Bennet's side.

"It is," Bennet replied, watching as his partner approached. "What are you doing here?"

Vaughn studied the privacy fence in front of them. "Gabby told Natalie all the details, and I was instructed to help or be excommunicated or something, and I'm not keen on arguing with a woman and a newborn. Three law enforcement officers are better than one. At least when they're the three of us."

"Then I don't have to brief you?"

"Alyssa is missing. We're likely dealing with the Dominguez and Jimenez cartels in some capacity. We have no idea who or what is in that house. That about cover it?"

"About," Bennet muttered, eyeing the privacy fence again. "The fence is weird, and I assume if this really is some kind of cartel headquarters or meeting place or whatever, it's got cameras everywhere."

"Likely," Jaime replied. "Gabby found me possible floor plans, though," he said, holding out his phone. "This was on the developer's website, and it looks about right. Now, we don't know what kind of modifications the owners might have made over the years, but it gives us an idea."

They each took a turn looking at the floor plan and committing what they could to memory.

"We don't know what kind of arsenal they have," Bennet said. He didn't mind risking himself, but he couldn't put these two men at risk like this. He needed their help, he knew that, but he couldn't risk their lives like this. "I want you two to stay back."

Vaughn scoffed and Jaime shook his head.

"Look, they could be watching for us. They could be armed. You really want to get your head blown off? You're supposed to get married soon," he said, pointing at Jaime. "And you just had a kid."

"We've both done raids, Bennet," Vaughn said.

"We know the risks, and the best practices. I've got a vest on. You?"

Jaime and Bennet nodded.

"So, we do what we'd do in any other situation. We're careful, but this is still our job. If something goes bad, it's the risk we took when we took those badges. And I think Natalie and Gabby would understand since they consider Alyssa their sister."

"Fine. We do this together, but I take the risks, you understand? I screwed this up, and I let her out of my sight. This is on me." Bennet knew Vaughn wanted to argue, but they didn't have time. "We'll split up to check the perimeter and see if there are any vulnerabilities in the fence. Vaughn, you stay here and watch for any comings and goings. Stay in the dark so no neighbors get worried and call the cops. Jaime, you take the east side. If they have a monitoring system, they won't know you as any different from a neighbor walking down the street. I'll start on this side, and we'll meet in the back. Understood?"

Vaughn had stiffened, and Bennet knew his partner well enough to know Vaughn didn't particularly care to take orders from him. But, Vaughn didn't argue. He and Jaime both nodded.

Which was all Bennet needed to take off. He walked down the fence that hid the side of the house, running his hands up and down the surface, trying to find a weakness. He'd brought a few tools when he'd started out in case he'd have to do some not-quite-lawful breaking and entering. If he could find a decent crack or opening, he could possibly pry a section open and sneak in undetected.

He had to believe they had the element of surprise on their side. They wouldn't expect him to figure out their hiding spot, at least not this quickly, but that didn't mean they weren't being diligent.

Bennet made it down the entire side of the house, and when he turned the corner, the shadow of Jaime was turning the one across from him.

Bennet was half-tempted to just blow a hole in the damn fence, but that'd probably draw unwanted attention, and he might as well go through the front if he was going to go down that route.

But there was something of a joint at the corner of the fence here. Where the side had been one long sheet of whatever material the fence was made out of, where they connected at the corner had something of a space. Oh, the materials butted up against each other and were clearly screwed together tightly, but Bennet had to believe with enough force he could pry it open.

Jaime crossed to him. "You're going to need a crowbar or something like it."

"Luckily, I came prepared to do a little breaking and entering." He'd had no trouble jamming the crowbar into his pocket. It had torn the fabric of the pocket, but the curved part of the tool had hooked onto his waistband well enough to keep it secured.

"Good thinking," Jaime said, looking around the

back. The house behind them had inside lights on, but none in the back to cast a light on them. Jaime positioned himself in front of Bennet so that if anyone did look out, they hopefully wouldn't notice a man crowbarring open a fence.

Of course, they might notice the tall, broad man just standing there, but Bennet couldn't worry about that. He shoved the sharp edge of the crowbar into the small space between joint and fence and worked to pull it apart.

It took longer than he wanted, but eventually the fence began to give, and once he'd separated the parts, he used his body weight to bend the joint enough he could step through and into the pitch-black of the backyard.

"I'm going in. Get Vaughn."

"And if they pick you off?"

"You know not to come this way, and you call in every law enforcement agency to handle the situation."

"We could do that right now, you know."

Bennet looked at the dark shadow of the house. "I can't risk her safety like that. If she's in there, if we let SWAT or some other high-handed assholes handle this, you know as well as I do she has less of a chance."

"Normally I'd argue with you."

"But you won't, will you?"

"No. I care about Alyssa, and apparently so do you. So, we'll do this our way first."

Bennet was already stepping through the space he'd made in the fence. He stayed close to the side fence, using it as a guide to bring him closer to the house.

There were no lights on, and with the moonlight hitting the upper half of the house, he could make out that there were no windows. Not one.

Interesting. He couldn't make out the bottom half of the house, but he could feel his way. He started at one edge and moved his body across the siding of the house until he felt the indentation of a door.

He paused, listening to the quiet of night. Nothing moved, no shots rang out, and if there *were* cameras on this side of the house, he didn't know how they'd be able to see anything.

He had a chance. He crouched next to the doorknob he'd felt out. He pulled out the tiny penlight from his pocket, followed by the lock-picking kit he'd shoved into his jacket pocket.

He heard Vaughn and Jaime quietly approach and went to work. If his picking the lock drew attention, ideally Jaime and Vaughn would have a chance to surprise anyone who came out.

He didn't care about his own safety right now. He'd gladly die if it meant they got Alyssa out of here in one piece.

Still, he pulled the gun out of his holster and placed

it next to his feet while he worked. He'd die for Alyssa in a heartbeat, but he wouldn't die without a fight.

SALVADOR HAD LEFT her and Oscar alone while he "readied his supplies," and Alyssa racked her brain for anything she could say to get through to her brother.

"They'll only kill you, too."

Oscar looked at her as though she were a fool. "I'm Dominguez's right-hand man. Not only will he protect me, but hundreds of men who work for us will, as well. CJ can't touch me. I'm nearly as powerful as him, and with Stevens in our pocket, it's only a matter of time before we use every law enforcement agency in Texas to take down the Jimenez cartel."

"Dad would be so disappointed in you."

"Dad doesn't know what century it is, Alyssa. He's completely gone."

"So, you're going to let this man rape and murder me?"

Oscar's throat worked for a few seconds before he turned away from her. He pressed his forehead to the concrete wall of the basement. "You don't understand, Lyss. I have to do this. I don't have a choice. Can't you understand the position CJ put me in?"

Alyssa opened her mouth to yell at him that she didn't care about CJ or Jimenez or anything, she just wanted to live, damn it, but the doorknob on the door across from her seemed to...make a noise.

Considering Oscar and Dominguez had appeared

from behind her, she could only assume this door led somewhere else. Maybe even outside?

Then the doorknob downright jiggled. She jerked her head to look at Oscar, but he didn't seem to notice, either in alarm or to go open it for anyone. Not with his head pressed to the wall.

Alyssa's heart leaped in hope. Maybe it was foolish to hope, but Bennet wouldn't give up. He'd do whatever it took. She knew he would, and if it was a chance...

"Can't you do one favor for me, Oscar?" she breathed, trying to sound sad and terrified instead of elated. "One last favor before you let me die?"

"It's not up to me, Alyssa," he said, sounding sad and resigned as he thunked his head against the concrete of the basement wall. Over and over. "I don't have a choice. You forgive me, don't you? You will. I think you will. Once you understand."

"Can't you bring me milk and cookies? One last time?" Even though it was a fake request, it caused a lump to rise in her throat, but she had to speak loudly enough that the increased shaking of the knob didn't get his attention. "Please, Oscar, I'll forgive you if you show me this one kindness."

Oscar turned slowly, and Alyssa forced herself to hold his gaze instead of looking at the jiggling knob. She had to keep his attention on her, or on the wall, but nowhere near that door.

"You will? Really?"

"I promise. I'll do whatever you want of me, if you just… Bring me milk and cookies like you used to."

Oscar swallowed and nodded slowly, then more quickly. "Okay. Okay, I mean, I doubt we've got milk and cookies, but I'll find a snack. A good one. He'll have to let me do that. A show of respect. It's a show of respect," he said, and leaned down to kiss her cheek.

She tried not to flinch, tried to smile tremulously as she squeezed her eyes shut, hoping a tear would fall over.

"A delicious snack coming right up," Oscar whispered, heading behind her where she couldn't see. She could only hope he'd have to leave the room they were in. She could only hope whoever was on the other side of that door was someone who could save her. Who would.

She heard the door open and close behind her and then prayed, fervently, for the shaking knob to do more than just shake.

"Please, please for the love of God," she whispered, watching the door and wishing with everything she had it would open and Bennet would be on the other side.

When that happened almost exactly as she imagined it, she nearly couldn't believe it. But the door opened with a click, slowly inching open, before Bennet appeared.

She nearly cried out with joy, swallowing it down at the last minute. Tears erupted, but she swallowed down the sobs. For a brief second Bennet kneeled there looking around the edge of the door as if shocked to see her, but then he was all action and movement before she could even register it.

He was at her feet, pulling the knife out of her bra before she could manage a word.

"Tell me everything you know," he whispered, the command calm and clear and helping to keep her focused.

"There're two men that I know of," she whispered as he began to cut all her ties quickly and efficiently. "Dominguez and Oscar. But I woke up right here so I don't know what's up there. Oscar's getting me a snack. Dominguez is getting what he needs to kill—"

The telltale sound of the door behind her squeaking open had her stopping, icy fear gripping her. They'd kill Bennet and then her and—

But the last of the ties fell off and Bennet shoved the knife into her hand as he pulled his gun. A shot fired and Alyssa cried out because she knew Bennet couldn't have fired yet. His gun clattered to the ground, and he stumbled back.

Alyssa clutched the knife in her hand, turning to see Salvador standing there, gun in each hand pointed at both of them. She tried to step in front of Bennet, but he was already on his feet, pushing her back behind *him*.

"Are all Rangers this stupid?" Salvador demanded, pointing both guns at Bennet. Bennet stood there, shirt ripped and blood dripping from where the bullet must have grazed. He was standing, though, looking defiant and pissed as ever, so Alyssa had to believe he was okay. She had to.

"Are all common criminals this stupid?" Bennet returned conversationally.

Salvador's laugh was low and horrible. Alyssa shuddered, trying to think. A knife didn't trump a gun, but maybe she could throw it? Maybe she could lure him close enough to...

"Oscar. Tie up the Ranger. He's going to be our audience, I think. Yes, I think he'll enjoy what I have planned for our little lady."

Bennet whistled, high and quick. Salvador frowned, and then a shot was fired from somewhere behind her and Bennet.

One of Salvador's guns clattered to the ground on a howl of outrage, red blooming near his elbow. "Oscar," he screamed. "Shoot them!"

"I... I left my gun in the kitchen," Oscar whispered, wide-eyed and terrified.

"You have three seconds to drop the weapon, Dominguez," a man from behind them ordered. Alyssa looked back, and her knees nearly gave out. Vaughn and Jaime were standing at the door, weapons trained on Salvador and Oscar.

Jaime began to count off. "Three, two—"

But Salvador grinned. Everything else after that awful, soul-freezing grin went too fast. The next thing Alyssa fully understood was Bennet on top of her and the sounds of at least two gunshots being fired.

"Bennet?" she managed, barely able to breathe between his crushing weight and the hard, cold concrete ground.

He groaned, and panic clutched her throat. She tried to get out his name again, but her throat felt paralyzed. *She* felt paralyzed.

"Vest," he finally wheezed, pushing off her.

"Vest?" she returned dumbly, but he was getting off her. He was standing up. He had to be okay. She rolled onto her back as he straightened to full height, looking a little too pale for her comfort. But he held out his hand as if she was supposed to take it.

She could only stare. Surely, he'd been shot, but he was standing there trying to help her up.

"You're one lucky bastard," Vaughn muttered, standing behind Bennet and studying his back. "That bullet isn't even an inch away from the edge."

Bennet merely grunted, now not waiting for her to find the wherewithal to grab his hand. He bent over and took her hand and tugged her onto her feet.

"Are you hurt?" he asked, his fingers curling around her shoulders as he studied her intently.

"You've been shot. Twice," she returned, staring at his gorgeous face, a little afraid this was all a dream.

"Yeah, and I'm still standing. Now, are you hurt?" he repeated, more forcefully this time.

"No. I mean, Oscar knocked me out, but—"

Bennet whirled around, but whatever he'd been about to do, Vaughn stepped in front of him.

"Let's let the law handle the rest of this."

That's when Alyssa finally felt like things were real. This had all happened. She looked over at Jaime, who stood above the two men who'd kidnapped her. Jaime was talking on his cell, Salvador laid out in a pile of blood, but his hands were cuffed behind his back as he lay there facedown, so it was possible he was still alive.

Oscar was in a sitting position, rocking back and forth, his hands also cuffed behind his back. Everything seemed to fade away at that moment except her brother.

Her brother who had knocked her out. Who had been a part of a plan to rape and kill her. Who had considered that *fine* because he wouldn't be the one doing it. All for revenge. All because CJ wouldn't respect him.

Alyssa pushed past Bennet. Whatever Vaughn and Bennet said to her, she didn't hear any of it. She stormed over to Oscar, who was looking up at her with tears in his eyes.

"I'm so sorry, Lyss. So sorry. Can't you forg—"

Alyssa didn't want to listen to another syllable, so she bent over and elbowed him in the nose as hard as she'd elbowed the man who'd tried to abduct her last week.

Oscar cried out, blood spurting from his nose.

"I *hate* you," she spat at him, a few tears spilling over her own cheeks. "And I'll never forgive you, you weak, soulless bastard." She turned away from him then, and Bennet was right there. Bleeding and beautiful.

"You saved me." It was all she could think to say, standing in this basement, surrounded by injured men and lawmen and this man. This wonderful man who had saved her from the worst thing she'd ever faced, and that was saying something.

His throat worked for a few seconds before he spoke. "I never should have let you out of my sight."

"But—"

Suddenly men were pouring through the door. Police and FBI, all talking and ordering things, radios squawking, paramedics jogging.

And somehow she was being led out of the basement, away from Bennet, too many questions being asked of her, too many hands prodding at her when all she wanted to do was cry in the comforting circle of Bennet's arms.

But he was still in that basement, not looking at her, and Alyssa realized she might have been saved, but nothing much had changed. He was still a Ranger, and she was still a Jimenez.

Nothing could change that.

Chapter Seventeen

Bennet was doing everything in his power not to shove the paramedic working on his arm. He didn't particularly feel like having his wounds tended to right now.

Nor did he feel like answering anyone's endless questions, not when Alyssa had been taken out of the basement that was now crawling with all manner of law enforcement.

"We're going to have to transport you, Ranger Stevens. Even a minor bullet wound is a bullet wound."

Bennet tried to make his face do anything other than scowl, but it was a lost cause. He didn't want to go to a damn hospital. He wanted to sit down and go through everything that had happened. Not with FBI or other Rangers or anyone. Just Alyssa.

Who had been led away and hadn't reappeared.

"I'll go see if the second ambulance is here, if you'll wait."

Bennet nodded, staring at the chair Alyssa had been tied to when he'd gotten inside. Tied up. *This* close to dying. Because of him and all the mistakes he'd made along the way.

Jaime reappeared from wherever he'd been outside. Bennet glanced up at the man who'd helped him. Bennet didn't know much what to say. What could be said when you'd made this kind of a mess of things?

"Paramedics checked Alyssa out, and she was cleared to go home. Vaughn is taking her back to his house. Gabby's there, and she'll take good care of her."

Bennet nodded. "They're going to make me go to the hospital."

"Bullet wounds will do that to you. I'll let Alyssa know once she's had some rest. Don't want her rushing off to the hospital."

Bennet laughed bitterly. "I'm the reason she was put in this position. I wouldn't worry about it."

"Come on, Bennet. We've both been doing this too long to talk like that."

"I let my guard down. I trusted the wrong people. She could have been killed."

"But she wasn't. You know those seconds matter. The end result matters. Justice matters in the end."

"It's different," Bennet said flatly, because some man he barely knew, no matter what help he'd offered, couldn't absolve this black cloud of guilt.

"Why? Because you're involved with her?"

When Bennet didn't respond in any way, because

yes he *had* been involved with her but he wasn't so certain he would be from here on out, Jaime continued.

"Been there, done that, buddy. It's really not different. Not when you've both survived relatively unscathed and have a chance to build a very nice future."

"She was knocked out, tied to a chair and seconds away from being killed. We must have different definitions of *unscathed*."

"We don't get out of life unscathed. Not a one of us. Alyssa's tough. She's had to be. If you think she's going to wither away—"

"I don't think that. I know she's tough. She's tougher than she should have to be, because she's had shit thrown at her her whole life."

"Then how about this? Don't be more of the shit. I didn't get to save Gabby when she was in trouble. She mostly saved herself. I didn't like it, but you know what I did like? Getting someone I loved and wanted to marry and have a family with out of the deal. So. Stop being a dumbass."

"Thanks for the pep talk," Bennet muttered as the paramedic reappeared.

"Go to the hospital. I'll let Alyssa know you'll be by when you're released. Don't disappoint her, or you'll have a whole slew of intimidating women to answer to."

Bennet nodded absently as Jaime went over to talk to another FBI agent and the paramedic started leading him out of the house.

He *was* being a dumbass, feeling sorry for himself, blaming himself, and as much as it felt right to wallow in that, Jaime had a point. This was over now, and Alyssa *was* safe.

There'd be fallout to deal with. His father was a part of this, and Bennet... He didn't know how to absorb that, or how she would. How anyone would.

But Alyssa was safe. Alive and safe and able to go home, and maybe she hated him a little bit now. He could deal with that. He could deal with any range of emotions she had toward him, but that didn't mean he had to sulk and give up and stay away.

Not when he'd fallen in love with her, and damn it if she wasn't tough enough to take it.

Alyssa had showered as much of the day off her as she could. She'd been fussed over by Gabby, had a newborn baby shoved into her arms and been plied with tea.

She hated tea, but she hadn't found her voice. Not since Vaughn had ushered her away from the house she'd been tied up in and driven her to his house.

Natalie and Gabby had done *all* the talking since then. It was nice, all in all, since Alyssa didn't know what to say or what to feel. Her entire body felt cold and numb.

A knock sounded at the door, and Vaughn disappeared to answer it. When he returned, Jaime was with him.

Alyssa had approximately eight thousand questions she wanted to ask him, but in the end she just looked down at the baby sleeping in her awkwardly positioned arms. The little girl was so tiny, her face all scrunched up in sleep.

Alyssa's chest felt too tight, her eyes too scratchy. Everything ached and hurt and didn't make any damn sense.

She swallowed at the lump in her throat, still watching the baby in her arms. "How is everything?" she managed to ask, her voice squeaky.

"Everyone has been transported to the hospital. In Bennet's and Oscar's cases that's more of a precaution than a necessity. I arranged to have your bike brought here, and it's out in the driveway." He placed her keys on the table next to the couch.

"Wait. You didn't give her a chance to talk to Bennet before you brought her home?" Natalie demanded, turning toward Vaughn.

"Bennet was a little busy. Would you sit down? You shouldn't be up around pacing."

"I'm not pacing, I was getting Alyssa more tea, and I will not sit down. Is your memory faulty?"

"Alyssa hasn't drunk the tea she's got and my memory is fine," Vaughn replied, pressing Natalie into the chair.

Natalie whipped her accusatory gaze to Jaime. "You, too?"

"He needed to be transported to the hospital. The entire place was crawling with law enforcement. That's not exactly the time to talk."

"Even though you both know talking after these kinds of ordeals is important?" Natalie returned.

But Alyssa had been glad. She didn't want to talk to Bennet just yet. Not when all she felt was this horrible numbness interrupted only intermittently by the need to cry. She wouldn't cry in front of him in the aftermath. She needed to be strong the next time she spoke to Bennet.

Strong enough to pretend she didn't care that they didn't have a future together.

"Bennet will be by once he's released," Jaime said. "They'll be able to talk in a calm, comforting environment instead of in the middle of a crime scene."

"Unless that's not what you want?" Gabby said, sliding onto the couch next to Alyssa. It was the first time in this conversation anyone had talked to Alyssa directly.

Which Alyssa wanted to shy away from. She wanted to live in this numb bubble for right now. She didn't want to think about Bennet or the impossibility of their future. She didn't want to think about Oscar or what he'd been willing to do. She didn't want to think of CJ killing her mother or any of it.

She just wanted to stare at a sweet little sleeping baby who would always know her parents loved her.

"We can tell him not to come, sweetie. Until you're ready." Gabby squeezed her arm, and Alyssa barely felt it. She wasn't sure she'd ever feel ready. What had she ever been ready for in her life? She'd only ever had things happen to her and learned to deal, or learned to fight, or learned to be the victim. Time and time again.

Something poked through all the numbness. Anger. She was so damn tired of being a *victim*. So tired of things happening to her and her having to learn how to fight, how to survive.

When was it going to be her turn to live? To make choices without worrying if she was going to inconvenience someone or get them connected to something they shouldn't be connected to. When did she get to have a *life*? With ups and downs and successes and failures and...

"Can you take her?" Alyssa asked abruptly, nodding toward the baby she was still afraid to jostle.

Gabby obliged and Alyssa stood as soon as she was free of the baby. "I have to go," she announced to no one in particular.

"You're not going anywhere, Alyssa."

Alyssa ignored Gabby. "What's happening with Gary Stevens?" she demanded of Jaime.

"He's been arrested. He has a team of lawyers working to get him released, but there's a lot of damning evidence to him being an accessory. Including Oscar's throwing him under the bus."

"And Dominguez?"

Jaime shoved his hands into his pockets, rocking back on his heels. "Died en route to the hospital."

"Good. And my brother?"

"Oscar is being checked out, and once he's fit for

confinement, he'll be transported to jail. We're also applying for warrants on your brother CJ in the murder of your mother."

"Oh." Alyssa cleared her throat. "Good. Good, I'm glad." They should all pay for what they'd done. Every last one of them. "I need to go then."

Jaime glanced at Gabby as if asking permission. Alyssa scowled. "I don't want to wait for him to get here. I have some things to say to him. I'm not waiting. I'm done with waiting."

Jaime inclined his head. "I can't argue with that. Can you?" he asked pointedly at Gabby.

Alyssa looked back at her friend, her *sister*—more her family than any of the horrible men related to her—and Gabby sighed heavily.

"Just drive her to the hospital."

"I can handle myself," Alyssa retorted.

"We all can, but it doesn't hurt to let the people who care about us take care of us either. Got it?"

That numbness receded further. Care and taking care. *That* was what she wanted out of her life. She crossed back to Gabby and gave her a hug. "Thank you," she whispered, then did the same to Natalie. "Thank you for being my family," she said firmly. Damn if she'd ever be afraid or hesitant to say that again.

"And I appreciate the taking care," she continued. "But this is something personal and I want to drive myself. Okay?"

Gabby gave a nod. "Just keep us informed on where you are so we don't worry, okay?"

"I will." Because that's what family did, and she was most definitely part of a real family now.

Chapter Eighteen

Bennet signed the paperwork to get him the hell out of the hospital. It shouldn't take that long to stitch up a little bullet wound, Bennet thought.

Captain Dean had debriefed him on the status of Alyssa's mother's murder case, including a warrant for CJ Jimenez. Bennet couldn't begin to guess what Alyssa would think of that when she'd been so certain her brothers hadn't done it.

But no matter how she took it, he wanted to be the one standing by her as she did. Now, he just had to hope she'd let him.

The nurse ushered him out of the room he'd been in, and when Bennet stepped into the waiting room, he stopped short. "Mother."

Mom stood from the chair she'd been sitting in. She'd changed out of her gala finery, and in fact looked pale and as mussed and bedraggled as he'd ever seen her in his entire life.

"Have you been released?" she asked as if she was asking him how the weather was.

"Yes."

Mom swallowed, clutching her purse in front of her. "The police are crawling all over my home and guesthouse. I'd relish the opportunity to stay away and drive my son back to his house." She swallowed, and Bennet realized no matter how calmly she spoke, she was as affected as her appearance might suggest.

Bennet sighed. "They arrested Dad?"

Mom nodded tersely. "Obviously his lawyers are working overtime to find some loophole."

Bennet didn't know what to say to that. Didn't know what to do with this. What he wanted was to see Alyssa, to talk to her, to sort things out, but maybe this was as important to sort out.

"I had no idea," Mom said, her voice more a whisper than that cool politician's tone she'd been employing. "Apparently his assistant was the only one who did. I don't know why he'd risk it, Bennet. Working with a cartel, no matter what the money, is political suicide."

"Unless no one finds out and you can use it to aid your cause."

Mom shook her head. "It's unconscionable. Maybe you don't believe me, maybe he could have convinced me otherwise, but I swear to you, if I had known... I would have had to have turned him in. My career is everything to me, Bennet. It always has been for better or worse, but I never could have condoned this kind of..." She shook her head, a tear slipping over her cheek.

It was impossible not to believe his mother at this point. She wasn't an emotional woman. She hadn't even cried at her own mother's funeral. For her to be this distraught, she had to be caught completely unaware, and he supposed as separate as his parents had been conducting their lives, it was more than possible.

"I'm sorry you got caught up in it."

Mom nodded jerkily. "You, as well. I hope Alyssa wasn't hurt."

"Not physically."

"Good. I… Well, I suppose I wasn't overly polite when I met her."

"Are you going to apologize how you treated a woman in my life, Mother?" Bennet asked incredulously.

Mom sniffed. "Well, it perhaps took my life being ruined before my eyes to get me to that point, but yes. And, though I'm sure you'll think it makes me cold and callous, your father's ruined our name completely now. It doesn't really matter what women you consort with at this point."

Perhaps it shouldn't be funny, but after this long-ass day, Bennet could only laugh. He laughed and did something he hadn't done for years, maybe over a decade.

He hugged his mother.

"Oh, well, it turns out you might be busy," Mom said after giving him a quick squeeze back. When he pulled away, his mother pointed to the doors of the waiting room.

Alyssa stood there, arms crossed over her chest, looking beautiful and pissed off. And for the first time since she'd shown him the gun strapped to her thigh just *hours* ago, he finally relaxed again.

She was here. They were both all right. If they could both survive a kidnapping plot orchestrated by members of each of their families, they could probably figure just about anything out.

"Go to my house. Stay there until the police clear out of yours. I have…business to take care of," Bennet told his mother absently.

"Bennet, I'm going to tell you something I'm likely never to admit aloud again."

"Yeah?"

"I quite like her."

He managed to tear his gaze away from Alyssa and stared at his mother, who shrugged and began walking for the exit. She paused as she approached Alyssa, said something, and then she was gone.

Then it was just the two of them. And a handful of people in the waiting room, but he barely noticed. He walked toward her, and she didn't move. Just stood there staring at him as though they were about to fight.

"They stitch you up?" she asked.

"Yes."

"And you're okay?"

"Aside from a bruise the size of Jupiter on my back and some stitches on my arm."

"Well, you got something to say to me?" She lifted her chin, all brave defiance, and he grinned.

"Yeah." But he didn't say any of it. He kissed her instead, tangling his fingers in her hair, drowning in the taste of her he'd never be able to live without no matter how he might fail her in the future.

ALYSSA HAD NOT come to the hospital to make out in the waiting room in front of a handful of people, but now that Bennet's arms were around her, his mouth on hers, it was hard to remember what she had planned to do.

She wanted to stay here, in this moment, for good. They were safe. They were together. He was *kissing* her regardless of her last name or his.

"Bennet," she murmured against his mouth. She'd come here with things to say. Things to demand, and he was dismantling it all because this was all that mattered. All she wanted. Him, him, him.

His hands moved to cup her cheeks, his mouth brushing across her mouth in between his words. "If you're going to yell at me, can it wait?"

"For what?"

He pressed his forehead to hers, his eyes still closed. "My wounds to heal, the case to be over, fifty years—take your pick."

"No, I didn't mean wait for what, I mean what would I yell at you for?"

His eyes opened, blue and vibrant. "You didn't come here to yell at me?"

"No, I came here to tell you that I'm tired of waiting and being pushed aside and we will talk about everything on *my* time, and when *I* want to."

"Okay," he returned all too reasonably.

"And I don't want to do it in this damn waiting room with all these people listening to me."

"Okay."

"And stop saying okay!"

He grinned at her again, and she didn't know whether to laugh or cry, tell him she loved him or kiss him a million times over no matter who they were in front of.

"All right," he said, feigning seriousness. "This is where I point out I don't have a car or any way of getting us out of here."

"I guess you'll have to ride on the back of my bike. If you think you're up to it."

"I guess it's fitting punishment all in all."

She frowned at him. "Why do you think I'm going to yell at you or you need to be punished? You recall saving my life earlier, right?"

"I'm the reason you were in that position. I let my father convince me to do something I knew I shouldn't. I didn't want to leave you with him. It went against every gut feeling I had, but I let it go because…"

"Because he's your father. You think I don't understand the way loyalty and family love can screw with you? I trusted Oscar. I trusted CJ. They… Bennet, you want to love your family, and it's an awful thing when they don't deserve it. But it's not our fault."

His thumb brushed her cheek, back and forth, and all she wanted was to be in a bed somewhere with him and shut the world and their families and this awful day away for good. But his next words made her breath catch.

"I love you," he said in the middle of a hospital waiting room, earnestly and looking her right in the eye as if there was no greater truth in the world.

Alyssa tried to make sense of those three simple words. Except, she hadn't expected them, and they were anything but simple. "Wh-what?"

"'What' as in you didn't hear me or you don't believe me or you don't want me to?"

"I…"

"Because I'm not sure how to talk you into loving me back without knowing which objection I'm fighting."

"You don't have to talk me into it," she managed to say through her tight, scratchy throat.

"I don't?"

"I may not have had very good luck with the kind of love a person is born with, but I've been pretty good about finding it myself these past few years." With shaky fingers, she traced the impressive cut of his jaw. "I love you, Bennet."

"Just took a week, a few kidnapping attempts and successes, a dramatic shootout."

"Don't forget the involvement of family members."

"No, who could forget that?" He inhaled deeply, then let it out. He looked at her so intently Alyssa wasn't sure she'd ever get used to it, but she'd gladly spend a very long time trying.

"We managed to turn today around, I think," he murmured, still touching her face, still looking at her in that heart-melting way.

Alyssa glanced at the clock. "It's after midnight. It's tomorrow."

"Even better."

Then he was kissing her in the middle of this waiting room again, and she didn't care anymore at all.

Epilogue

One Year Later

"The timing is so funny," Tawny said, attaching a golden hairpiece to Alyssa's impossibly perfect updo. "I swear we were just doing this a year ago."

"We were," Alyssa returned. "Except I was wearing black."

"And now you look positively radiant in white." Tawny stepped back and studied her handiwork. "Please wear the heels. Please. I beg of you."

"Sorry. Tennis shoes are tradition."

"So is kidnapping. I'm hoping we avoid that this time around."

"You and me both."

Tawny pouted at Alyssa's feet. "Well, at least they're white. But everyone is going to see them when you walk down the aisle."

"They'll survive the shock."

"Ready for the great unveiling?" Tawny asked.

Alyssa took stock of herself in the mirror. It was

no different from how she'd felt a year ago getting ready for a Christmas gala, and yet it was completely different. As uncomfortable as she felt all dressed up, she was going to her wedding this time.

And that made all the difference in the world.

Tawny opened the bathroom door and ushered her out into the bedroom where the photographer and her bridesmaids waited. Natalie and Gabby were both dressed in beautiful forest green, Nat holding pretty little Sarah dressed in red toddler finery on her hip, Gabby lying miserably on the bed.

But both looked at Alyssa as she entered the room, brown eyes shiny.

"Oh, you look like a princess," Natalie said with a little sniffle. "It's perfect."

"You look great, Lyss," Gabby added. "I've got a bet with Jaime that Bennet cries, so do your best for me, okay?"

Alyssa managed a laugh, feeling a little teary herself. "You going to make it down the aisle?"

"Do you want me to go get you some ginger ale?" Tawny asked.

"No, I'd prefer a time machine so I can fast-forward out of morning sickness land," Gabby replied.

"You're getting there," Nat offered.

Gabby simply groaned, but Alyssa had to grin. She'd spent much of her life alone and isolated, and now she was getting married surrounded by her surrogate family. Her sisters, her friends. And soon enough she'd be walking down the aisle to the man she loved.

She swallowed at the lump in her throat, because she did not want to go through the arduous process of redoing her makeup.

A knock sounded at the door, and when Tawny opened it she screeched and slammed it right back shut. "You are not supposed to see the bride, Bennet Stevens," she scolded through the door.

"I'm not superstitious," Bennet returned from behind the closed door.

"Well, I am," Alyssa said, crossing to the door. "So get the hell out of here."

"Open the door."

"No."

"Just a crack. We don't have to see each other. I just want to give you something."

"If it's jewelry, I don't want it."

"It's not jewelry. Open the door and hold out your damn hand, woman."

She looked at the door, unable to stop grinning. How she'd gotten here, she'd never know, but she was so happy. So, so happy, and what's more, she knew she darn well deserved it.

She cracked the door open and stuck her hand out the crack. Bennet placed something in her palm, and she curled her fingers around the slim piece of metal and pulled it to her.

When she uncurled her fingers, she was staring at

a Swiss Army knife. A *monogrammed* Swiss Army knife, with her soon-to-be initials on it.

"If I'm not fishing that out of your dress later, you're going to be in very big trouble," Bennet said from behind the door.

Tawny peered into Alyssa's palm and wrinkled her nose. "What kind of gift is a *knife*?"

Alyssa slid the knife into the top of her dress, making sure it was secure before she flashed a grin at Tawny. "The perfect gift." She cleared her throat and peeked out the crack in the door.

Bennet was standing there looking all too pleased with himself, polished and perfect in his tux.

She kept her body hidden behind the door, but stuck her head out the crack.

"Hi," he offered.

"Hi," she returned. She stuck her finger out the crack and crooked it at him so he'd step closer.

"If I come closer, I'm going to kiss you," he warned.

"On the cheek," she said, offering her cheek, but as he moved closer, he only cupped her face with his hands and bent his face close enough their noses were touching.

"Not the cheek," he whispered, touching his lips to hers. It would ruin her lipstick, but she was a little too happy to care. She kissed him right back.

There were protests from inside, but Alyssa didn't care. Today she was marrying the man she loved, and no luck—good or bad—could stand in her way.

"I love you, Ranger Stevens," she murmured against his mouth.

"And I love you." He pulled away, that charming grin firmly in place. "See you soon, wife," he offered, heading back down the hall toward the grand staircase. They would be getting married at the bottom of it, then having their reception in the huge living room decorated with the giant gold tree she'd admired last year.

Bennet hadn't loved the idea of getting married at the Stevenses' house, what with his father being in jail, but Alyssa thought it was fitting. It was where they'd had their first real kiss, where they'd made love for the first time, where they'd spent all that time together that had led them to this wonderful moment.

Yes, it was perfect, even in all its glitz and glamour, and when they went home tonight to Bennet's less flashy house that he'd insisted she help decorate over the past few months, they'd have their low-key, very naked wedding night, and celebrate the start of a very wonderful, *loving* life together.

And if everything in her life had led her to this wonderful point, she wouldn't trade any of it and risk missing out on that. Because the life she'd built in her newfound freedom wasn't perfect, but it was full of love, and love, it turned out, wasn't a weapon.

It was freedom.

* * * * *

I N T R I G U E

Available October 17, 2017

#1743 SHADOWS IN THE NIGHT
The Finnegan Connection • by Heather Graham
FBI special agent Micah Fox isn't accustomed to working with civilians, but criminologist Harley Frasier may be the next target after her mentor is murdered in this pulse-pounding new thriller from *New York Times* bestselling author Heather Graham.

#1744 COLTON K-9 COP
The Coltons of Shadow Creek • by Addison Fox
It isn't easy for quiet accountant Bellamy Reeves to open herself to trust, but she might have to make an exception for K-9 bomb squad officer Donovan Colton and his adorable dog when her life threatens to explode—literally.

#1745 DADDY DEFENDER
Omega Sector: Under Siege • by Janie Crouch
Someone has placed widow Summer Worrall and her small daughter in their crosshairs...but lucky for Summer, Ashton Fitzgerald isn't the handsome and unassuming handyman she thought he was. He's a highly trained sharpshooter intent on keeping his found family safe.

#1746 RELUCTANT HERO
by Debra Webb & Regan Black
It's bad enough for a security expert to be threatened over gold stolen during his unit's last mission in Iraq—a theft of which he's innocent. But to make matters worse, reporter Rebecca Wallace comes in harm's way while investigating him. Can he keep her safe and maintain his innocence in the line of fire?

#1747 MR. TAKEN
Mystery Christmas • by Danica Winters
Firefighter Colter Fitzgerald knows that Whitney Barstow has been burned in the past, but when Dunrovin ranch is targeted by an arsonist, can she face the fires of his passion? Or will their future go up in smoke?

#1748 SMALL-TOWN FACE-OFF
The Protectors of Riker County • by Tyler Anne Snell
Mara Copeland was born and raised in a world of criminals, so how could she face a future with Sheriff Billy Reed? But when she returns to Riker County with a child in her arms and trouble in hot pursuit, it's time to see where allegiances really lie...

Get 2 Free Books,
Plus 2 Free Gifts—
just for trying the Reader Service!

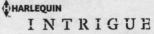

SPECIAL EXCERPT FROM

mira

*Special agent Griffin Price and historian Vickie Preston
are on their way to start a new life together. But a romantic
weekend detour is interrupted when a popular author
is found dead under mysterious circumstances in the
basement of a local restaurant, and the FBI's Krewe of
Hunters paranormal team is brought in to investigate…*

*Read on for a sneak preview of
WICKED DEEDS,
the next installment in the **KREWE OF HUNTERS** series
from New York Times bestselling author*
Heather Graham.

Vickie reached out and set her hand over Monica's. "I'm so sorry."

Monica Verne looked at Vickie and nodded. Griffin thought that Vickie's ability to feel with others and offer them real comfort was going to be one of her greatest assets in joining the Krewe. It was also going to be one of the most difficult parts of the job for her to learn to manage. He lowered his head for a moment; it was an odd time to smile. And an odd time to think just how lucky he was. Vickie was beautiful to look at—five foot eight, with long raven black waves of hair and blue-green eyes that could change and shimmer like emeralds.

She was also so caring—honest and filled with integrity.

He truly loved her. Watching her empathy and gentle touch with Monica, he knew all the more reason why.

"My husband didn't kill himself!" Monica whispered fervently.

"I don't think it's been suggested that he killed himself.

I believe they're considering it an accidental death," Griffin began.

"Accidental death, my ass! If there's any last thing I can do for Franklin, it's going to be to make someone prove that this was no accidental death!" Monica lashed out, indignant. She wasn't angry with Vickie—who was still holding her hand. Her passion was against the very suggestion that her husband's death had been through a simple slip—some misfortune.

She wagged a finger at Griffin. "You listen to me, and listen well. We were the best, Frankie and me. I swear it. When all else fell to hell and ruin, we still had one another… Franklin did not meet up with a friend! He did not break into that cellar to drink himself to death! I'm telling you, I knew my husband, he…"

She broke off, gritting her teeth. She was trying not to cry. The woman was truly in anguish; she was also furious.

"I don't know when he went out. I don't know why he went out—or how he wound up at the restaurant. I do know one thing."

"What is that, Mrs. Verne?" Vickie asked.

Monica Verne startled them both, slamming a fist on the coffee table. "My husband was murdered!"

The motion seemed to be a cue.

In the yard, a dozen birds took flight, shrieking and cawing.

Griffin could see them as they let out their cries, sweeping into the sky.

A murder of crows…

And an unkindness of ravens…

As poetically cruel as the death of Franklin Verne.

WICKED DEEDS
by New York Times *bestselling author Heather Graham.*
Available now from MIRA® Books.

www.Harlequin.com

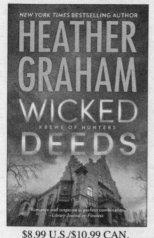

$8.99 U.S./$10.99 CAN.

$1.⁰⁰ OFF

New York Times bestselling author

HEATHER GRAHAM

returns with the next
action-packed romantic suspense story
in the *Krewe of Hunters* series.

WICKED DEEDS

Available now.

Harlequin.com

$1.⁰⁰ OFF the purchase price of WICKED DEEDS
by Heather Graham.

Offer valid from September 19, 2017, to October 31, 2017.
Redeemable at participating retail outlets, in-store only. Not redeemable at
Barnes & Noble. Limit one coupon per purchase. Valid in the U.S.A. and Canada only.

52615115

5 65373 00076 2   (8100)0 12306

® and ™ are trademarks owned and used by the trademark owner and/or its licensee.

© 2017 Harlequin Enterprises Limited

MCOUPHG1017

She prayed for sleep, but her mind kept returning to that time in the Sahara. Being part of the expedition had been such a privilege. She remembered the way they'd all felt when they'd broken through to the tomb. Satima Mahmoud—the pretty Egyptian interpreter who had so enchanted Joe Rosello—had been the first to scream when the workers found the entry.

Of course, Henry Tomlinson was called then. He'd been there to break the seal. They'd all laughed and joked about the curses that came with such finds, about the stupid movies that had been made.

Yes, people had died during other expeditions—as if they had been cursed. The Tut story was one example—and yet, by all accounts, there had been scientific explanations for everything that'd happened.

Almost everything, anyway.

And their find…

There hadn't been any curses. Not written curses, at any rate.

But Henry had died. And Henry had broken the seal…

No mummy curse had gotten to them; someone had killed Henry. And that someone had gotten away with it because neither the American Department of State nor the Egyptian government had wanted the expedition caught in the crosshairs of an insurgency. Reasonably enough!

But now…

For some reason, the uneasy dreams that came with her restless sleep weren't filled with mummies, tombs, sarcophagi or canopic jars. No funerary objects whatsoever, no golden scepters, no jewelry, no treasures.

Instead, she saw the sand. The endless sand of the Sahara. And the sand was teeming, rising up from the ground, swirling in the air.

Someone was coming…

She braced, because there were rumors swirling along with the sand. Their group could fall under attack—there was unrest in the area. Good Lord, they were in the Middle East!

But she found herself walking through the sand, toward whomever or whatever was coming.

She saw someone.

The killer?

She kept walking toward him. There was more upheaval behind the man, sand billowing dark and heavy like a twister of deadly granules.

Then she saw him.

And it was Micah Fox.

She woke with a start.

And she wondered if he was going to be her salvation…

Or a greater danger to her heart, a danger she hadn't yet seen.

Don't miss
SHADOWS IN THE NIGHT,
available November 2017 wherever
Harlequin® Intrigue books and ebooks are sold.

www.Harlequin.com

Need an adrenaline rush from nail-biting tales
(and irresistible males)?

Check out **Harlequin® Intrigue®**
and **Harlequin® Romantic Suspense** books!

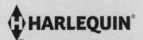